Penguin Modern Classics
The Unvanquished

William Faulkner was born near Oxford, Mississippi, in 1897. His great-grandfather, Colonel William Falkner (sic) had been one of the wild characters of the American South. The author, who had made little impression at school, was rejected by the U.S. army when America entered the First World War but became a pilot in the Canadian Flying Corps. After the war he attended the University of Mississippi for a time and then supported himself for several years through a variety of odd jobs, at the same time starting to write. While working in New Orleans he met the novelist Sherwood Anderson and through his encouragement wrote his first novel, *Soldier's Pay* (1926, Penguin 1938). This was followed by *Mosquitoes* (1927), a mildly satirical novel on New Orleans literary bohemia. Then, on Sherwood Anderson's advice, Faulkner turned to writing about his home area. *Sartoris* (1929), published in the year of his marriage, begins his famous series of novels and stories set in 'Yoknapatawpha County', north Mississippi. Although regional in setting, the Yoknapatawpha series continually draws the reader into the realm of myth, expressing a powerful imaginative vision of the human condition.

Other titles in this series include *The Sound and the Fury* (1929), *As I Lay Dying* (1930), *Sanctuary* (1931), *Light in August* (1932), *Absalom, Absalom!* (1936), *Go Down, Moses* (1942), *Intruder in the Dust* (1948), *Requiem for a Nun* (1951) and his last novel, *The Reivers* (1962). All of these are published by Penguin, as is his novel *The Wild Palms* (1939), and *The Portable Faulkner*, a chronological selection of Yoknapatawpha material edited by Malcolm Cowley.

Faulkner wrote poetry and many short stories as well as novels, and also worked on scripts for Hollywood as a way of making some money. Not long before his death in 1962 he moved his home to Charlottesville, Virginia. He was awarded the Nobel Prize for Literature in 1949 and in his speech reaffirmed the values that are voiced in his work: 'courage and honour and hope and pride and compassion and pity and sacrifice'.

The Unvanquished

William Faulkner

Penguin Books

in association with Chatto & Windus

PENGUIN BOOKS

Published by the Penguin Group
27 Wrights Lane, London w8 5tz, England
Viking Penguin Inc., 40 West 23rd Street, New York, New York 10010, USA
Penguin Books Australia Ltd, Ringwood, Victoria, Australia
Penguin Books Canada Ltd, 2801 John Street, Markham, Ontario, Canada l3r 1b4
Penguin Books (NZ) Ltd, 182–190 Wairau Road, Auckland 10, New Zealand

Penguin Books Ltd, Registered Offices: Harmondsworth, Middlesex, England

First published 1938
First published in Penguin Books 1955
Reprinted 1965, 1970, 1975, 1982, 1984, 1988

Set, printed and bound in Great Britain by
Cox & Wyman Ltd, Reading
Set in Monotype Garamond

Contents

Ambuscade

I

Behind the smokehouse that summer, Ringo and I had a living map. Although Vicksburg was just a handful of chips from the woodpile and the River a trench scraped into the packed earth with the point of a hoe, it (river, city, and terrain) lived, possessing even in miniature that ponderable though passive recalcitrance of topography which outweighs artillery, against which the most brilliant of victories and the most tragic of defeats are but the loud noises of a moment. To Ringo and me it lived, if only because of the fact that the sunimpacted ground drank water faster than we could fetch it from the well, the very setting of the stage for conflict a prolonged and wellnigh hopeless ordeal in which we ran, panting and interminable, with the leaking bucket between wellhouse and battlefield, the two of us needing first to join forces and spend ourselves against a common enemy, time, before we could engender between us and hold intact the pattern of recapitulant mimic furious victory like a cloth, a shield between ourselves and reality, between us and fact and doom. This afternoon it seemed as if we would never get it filled, wet enough, since there had not even been dew in three weeks. But at last it was damp enough, damp-coloured enough at least, and we could begin. We were just about to begin. Then suddenly Loosh w٠٠ standing there, watching us. He was Joby's son and Ringo's ٠٠cle; he stood there (we did not know where he had come from; we had not seen him appear, emerge) in the fierce dull early afternoon sunlight, bareheaded, his head slanted a little, tilted a little yet firm and not askew, like a cannonball (which it resembled) bedded hurriedly and carelessly in concrete, his eyes a little red at the inner corners as Negroes' eyes get when they have been drinking, looking down at what Ringo and I called Vicksburg. Then I saw Philadelphy, his wife, over at the woodpile, stooped, with an armful of wood already gathered into the crook of her elbow, watching Loosh's back.

'What's that?' Loosh said.

'Vicksburg,' I said.

Loosh laughed. He stood there laughing, not loud, looking at the chips.

'Come on here, Loosh,' Philadelphy said from the woodpile. There was something curious in her voice too – urgent, perhaps frightened. 'If you wants any supper, you better tote me some wood.' But I didn't know which, urgency or fright; I didn't have time to wonder or speculate, because suddenly Loosh stooped before Ringo or I could have moved, and with his hand he swept the chips flat.

'There's your Vicksburg,' he said.

'Loosh!' Philadelphy said. But Loosh squatted, looking at me with that expression on his face. I was just twelve then: I didn't know triumph; I didn't even know the word.

'And I tell you nother un you ain't know,' he said. 'Corinth.'

'Corinth?' I said. Philadelphy had dropped the wood and she was coming fast towards us. 'That's in Mississippi too. That's not far. I've been there.'

'Far don't matter,' Loosh said. Now he sounded as if he were about to chant, to sing; squatting there with the fierce dull sun on his iron skull and the flattening slant of his nose, he was not looking at me or Ringo either; it was as if his red-cornered eyes had reversed in his skull and it was the blank flat obverses of the balls which we saw. 'Far don't matter. Case hit's on the way!'

'On the way? On the way to what?'

'Ask your paw. Ask Marse John.'

'He's at Tennessee, fighting. I can't ask him.'

'You think he at Tennessee? Ain't no need for him at Tennessee now.' Then Philadelphy grabbed him by the arm.

'Hush your mouth, nigger!' she cried, in that tense desperate voice. 'Come on here and get me some wood!'

Then they were gone. Ringo and I didn't watch them go. We stood there above our ruined Vicksburg, our tedious hoe-scratch not even damp-coloured now, looking at one another quietly. 'What?' Ringo said, 'What he mean?'

'Nothing,' I said. I stooped and set Vicksburg up again. 'There it is.'

But Ringo didn't move, he just looked at me. 'Loosh

laughed. He say Corinth too. He laughed at Corinth too. What you reckon he know that we ain't?'

'Nothing!' I said. 'Do you reckon Loosh knows anything that Father don't know?'

'Marse John at Tennessee. Maybe he ain't know either.'

'Do you reckon he'd be away off at Tennessee if there were Yankees at Corinth? Do you reckon that if there were Yankees at Corinth, Father and General Van Dorn and General Pemberton all three wouldn't be there too?' But I was just talking too, I knew that, because niggers know, they know things; it would have to be something louder, much louder, than words to do any good. So I stooped and caught both hands full of dust and rose: and Ringo still standing there, not moving, just looking at me even as I flung the dust. 'I'm General Pemberton!' I cried. 'Yaaay! Yaay!' stooping and catching up more dust and flinging that too. Still Ringo didn't move. 'All right!' I cried. 'I'll be Grant this time, then. You can be General Pemberton.' Because it was that urgent, since Negroes knew. The arrangement was that I would be General Pemberton twice in succession and Ringo would be Grant, then I would have to be Grant once so Ringo could be General Pemberton or he wouldn't play any more. But now it was that urgent even though Ringo was a nigger too, because Ringo and I had been born in the same month and had both fed at the same breast and had slept together and eaten together for so long that Ringo called Granny 'Granny' just like I did, until maybe he wasn't a nigger any more or maybe I wasn't a white boy any more, the two of us neither, not even people any longer: the two supreme undefeated like two moths, two feathers riding above a hurricane. So we were both at it; we didn't see Louvinia, Joby's wife and Ringo's grandmother, at all. We were facing one another at scarcely arms' length, to the other each invisible in the furious slow jerking of the flung dust, yelling 'Kill the bastuds! Kill them! Kill them!' when her voice seemed to descend upon us like an enormous hand, flattening the very dust which we had raised, leaving us now visible to one another, dust-coloured ourselves to the eyes and still in the act of throwing:

'You, Bayard! You, Ringo!' She stood about ten feet away, her mouth still open with shouting. I noticed that she did not

now have on the old hat of Father's which she wore on top of
her head rag even when she just stepped out of the kitchen for
wood. 'What was that word?' she said. 'What did I hear you
say?' Only she didn't wait to be answered, and then I saw that
she had been running too. 'Look who coming up the big road!'
she said.

We – Ringo and I – ran as one, in midstride out of frozen
immobility, across the back yard and round the house, where
Granny was standing at the top of the front steps and where
Loosh had just come round the house from the other side and
stopped, looking down the drive towards the gate. In the
spring, when Father came home that time, Ringo and I ran
down the drive to meet him and return, I standing in one
stirrup with Father's arm around me, and Ringo holding to the
other stirrup and running beside the horse. But this time we
didn't. I mounted the steps and stood beside Granny, and with
Ringo and Loosh on the ground below the gallery we watched
the claybank stallion enter the gate which was never closed
now, and come up the drive. We watched them – the big gaunt
horse almost the colour of smoke, lighter in colour than the
dust which had gathered and caked on his wet hide where they
had crossed at the ford three miles away, coming up the drive
at a steady gait which was not a walk and not a run, as if he had
held it all the way from Tennessee because there was a need to
encompass earth which abrogated sleep or rest and relegated to
some insulated bourn of perennial and pointless holiday so
trivial a thing as galloping; and Father damp too from the ford,
his boots dark and dustcaked too, the skirts of his weathered
grey coat shades darker than the breast and back and sleeves
where the tarnished buttons and the frayed braid of his field
officer's rank glinted dully, the sabre hanging loose yet rigid at
his side as if it were too heavy to jounce or perhaps were at-
tached to the living thigh itself and took no more motion from
the horse than he did. He stopped; he looked at Granny and me
on the porch and at Ringo and Loosh on the ground.

'Well, Miss Rosa,' he said. 'Well, boys.'

'Well, John,' Granny said. Loosh came and took Jupiter's
head; Father dismounted stiffly, the sabre clashing dully and
heavily against his wet boot and leg.

'Curry him,' Father said. 'Give him a good feed, but don't turn him into the pasture. Let him stay in the lot . . . Go with Loosh,' he said, as if Jupiter were a child, slapping him on the flank as Loosh led him on. Then we could see him good. I mean, Father. He was not big; it was just the things he did, that we knew he was doing, had been doing in Virginia and Tennessee, that made him seem big to us. There were others besides him that were doing the things, the same things, but maybe it was because he was the only one we knew, had ever heard snoring at night in a quiet house, had watched eating, had heard when he talked, knew how he liked to sleep and what he liked to eat and how he liked to talk. He was not big, yet somehow he looked even smaller on the horse than off him, because Jupiter was big and when you thought of Father you thought of him as being big too and so when you thought of Father being on Jupiter it was as if you said, 'Together they will be too big; you won't believe it.' So you didn't believe it and so it wasn't. He came towards the steps and began to mount, the sabre heavy and flat at his side. Then I began to smell it again, like each time he returned, like the day back in the spring when I rode up the drive standing in one of his stirrups – that odour in his clothes and beard and flesh too which I believed was the smell of powder and glory, the elected victorious but know better now: know now to have been only the will to endure, a sardonic and even humorous declining of self-delusion which is not even kin to that optimism which believes that that which is about to happen to us can possibly be the worst which we can suffer. He mounted four of the steps, the sabre (that's how tall he actually was) striking against each one of the steps as he mounted, then he stopped and removed his hat. And that's what I mean: about his doing bigger things than he was. He could have stood on the same level with Granny and he would have only needed to bend his head a little for her to kiss him. But he didn't. He stopped two steps below her, with his head bared and his forehead held for her to touch her lips to, and the fact that Granny had to stoop a little now took nothing from the illusion of height and size which he wore for us at least.

'I've been expecting you,' Granny said.

'Ah,' Father said. Then he looked at me, who was still

looking at him, as Ringo at the foot of the steps beneath still was.

'You rode hard from Tennessee,' I said.

'Ah,' Father said again.

'Tennessee sho gaunted you,' Ringo said. 'What does they eat up there, Marse John? Does they eat the same things that folks eat?'

Then I said it, looking him in the face while he looked at me: 'Loosh says you haven't been at Tennessee.'

'Loosh?' Father said. 'Loosh?'

'Come in,' Granny said. 'Louvinia is putting your dinner on the table. You will just have time to wash.'

2

That afternoon we built the stock pen. We built it deep in the creek bottom, where you could not have found it unless you had known where to look, and you could not have seen it until you came to the new sap-sweating, axe-ended rails woven through and into the jungle growth itself. We were all there – Father and Joby and Ringo and Loosh and me – Father in the boots still but with his coat off now, so that we saw for the first time that his trousers were not Confederate ones but were Yankee ones, of new strong blue cloth, which they (he and his troop) had captured, and without the sabre now too. We worked fast, felling the saplings – the willow and pin oak, the swamp maple and chinkapin – and, without even waiting hardly to trim them, dragging them behind the mules and by hand too, through the mud and the briers to where Father waited. And that was it too; Father was everywhere, with a sapling under each arm going through the brush and briers almost faster than the mules; racking the rails into place while Joby and Loosh were still arguing about which end of the rail went where. That was it: not that Father worked faster and harder than anyone else, even though you do look bigger (to twelve, at least, to me and Ringo at twelve, at least) standing still and saying, 'Do this or that' to the ones who are doing; it was the way he did it. When he sat at his old place at the table in the dining-room and finished the side meat and greens and the cornbread and milk which Louvinia brought him (and we watching and waiting, Ringo and I at least, waiting for night and the talking, the telling) and wiped his beard and said, 'Now we're going to build a new pen. We'll have to cut the rails, too'; when he said that, Ringo and I probably had exactly the same vision. There would be all of us there – Joby and Loosh and Ringo and me on the edge of the bottom and drawn up into a kind of order – an order partaking not of any lusting and sweating for assault or even victory, but rather of that passive yet dynamic affirmation which Napoleon's troops must have felt – and facing us, between us and the bottom, between us and the waiting sap-running boles which were about to be transposed into dead rails, Father. He was on Jupiter now; he wore the frogged grey field officer's tunic; and while we watched he drew the sabre. Giving us a last embracing and comprehensive glance he drew it, already pivoting Jupiter on the tight snaffle; his hair tossed beneath the cocked hat, the sabre flashed and glinted; he cried, not loud yet stentorian: 'Trot! Canter! Charge!' Then, without even having to move, we could both watch and follow him – the little man (who in conjunction with the horse looked exactly the right size because that was as big as he needed to look and – to twelve years old – bigger than most folks could hope to look) standing in the stirrups above the smoke-coloured diminishing thunderbolt, beneath the arcy and myriad glitter of the sabre from which the chosen saplings, sheared, trimmed, and lopped, sprang into neat and waiting windrows, requiring only the carrying and the placing to become a fence.

The sun had gone out of the bottom when we finished the fence, that is, left Joby and Loosh with the last three panels to put up, but it was still shining up the slope of the pasture when we rode across it, I behind Father on one of the mules and Ringo on the other one. But it was gone even from the pasture by the time I had left Father at the house and returned to the stable, where Ringo already had a lead rope on the cow. So we went back to the new pen, with the calf following nuzzling and prodding at the cow every time she stopped to snatch a mouthful of grass, and the sow trotting on ahead. She (the sow) was the one who moved slow. She seemed to be moving slower than the cow even while the cow was stopped with Ringo leaned to the

taut jerk of the rope and hollering at the cow, so it was dark
sure enough when we reached the new pen. But there was still
plenty of gap left to drive the stock through. But then, we never
had worried about that.

We drove them in – the two mules, the cow and calf, the sow;
we put up the last panel by feel, and went back to the house. It
was full dark now, even in the pasture; we could see the lamp
in the kitchen and the shadow of someone moving across the
window. When Ringo and I came in, Louvinia was just closing
one of the big trunks from the attic, which hadn't been downstairs since the Christmas four years ago which we spent at
Hawkhurst, when there wasn't any war and Uncle Dennison
was still alive. It was a big trunk and heavy even when empty;
it had not been in the kitchen when we left to build the pen so it
had been fetched down some time during the afternoon, while
Joby and Loosh were in the bottom and nobody there to carry
it down but Granny and Louvinia, and then Father later, after
we came back to the house on the mule, so that was a part of the
need and urgency too; maybe it was Father who carried the
trunk down from the attic too. And when I went in to supper,
the table was set with the kitchen knives and forks in place of
the silver ones, and the sideboard (on which the silver service
had been sitting when I began to remember and where it had
been sitting ever since except on each Tuesday afternoon, when
Granny and Louvinia and Philadelphy would polish it, why,
nobody except Granny maybe knew, since it was never used)
was bare.

It didn't take us long to eat. Father had already eaten once
early in the afternoon, and besides that was what Ringo and I
were waiting for: for after supper, the hour of laxed muscles
and full entrails, the talking. In the spring when he came home
that time, we waited as we did now, until he was sitting in his
old chair with the hickory logs popping and snapping on the
hearth and Ringo and I squatting on either side of the hearth,
beneath the mantel above which the captured musket which he
had brought home from Virginia two years ago rested on two
pegs, loaded and oiled for service. Then we listened. We heard:
the names – Forrest and Morgan and Barksdale and Van Dorn;
the words like Gap and Run which we didn't have in Mississippi

even though we did own Barksdale, and Van Dorn until somebody's husband killed him, and one day General Forrest rode
down South Street in Oxford where there watched him through
a window pane a young girl who scratched her name on it with
a diamond ring: Celia Cook.

But we were just twelve; we didn't listen to that. What
Ringo and I heard was the cannon and the flags and the anony-
mous yelling. That's what we intended to hear tonight. Ringo
was waiting for me in the hall; we waited until Father was
settled in his chair in the room which he and the Negroes called
the Office – Father because his desk was here in which he kept
the seed cotton and corn and in this room he would remove his
muddy boots and sit in his stocking feet while the boots dried
on the hearth and where the dogs could come and go with
impunity, to lie on the rug before the fire or even to sleep there
on the cold nights – these whether Mother, who died when I
was born, gave him this dispensation before she died or whether
Granny carried it on afterward or whether Granny gave him
the dispensation herself because Mother died I don't know: and
the Negroes called the Office because into this room they
would be fetched to face the Patroller (sitting in one of the
straight hard chairs and smoking one of Father's cigars too but
with his hat off) and swear that they could not possibly have
been either whom or where he (the Patroller) said they were –
and which Granny called the library because there was one
bookcase in it containing a Coke upon Littleton, a Josephus, a
Koran, a volume of Mississippi Reports dated 1848, a Jeremy
Taylor, a Napoleon's Maxims, a thousand and ninety-eight
page treatise on astrology, a History of Werewolf Men in
England, Ireland and Scotland and including Wales by the
Reverend Ptolemy Thorndyke, M.A.(Edinburgh), F.R.S.S., a
complete Walter Scott, a complete Fenimore Cooper, a paper-
bound Dumas complete, too, save for the volume which Father
lost from his pocket at Manassas (retreating, he said).

So Ringo and I squatted again and waited quietly while
Granny sewed beside the lamp on the table and Father sat in
his old chair in its old place, his muddy boots crossed and lifted
into the old heel-marks beside the cold and empty fireplace,
chewing the tobacco which Joby had loaned him. Joby was a

good deal older than Father. He was too old to have been caught short of tobacco just by a war. He had come to Mississippi from Carolina with Father and he had been Father's body servant all the time that he was raising and training Simon, Ringo's father, to take over when he (Joby) got too old, which was to have been some years yet except for the War. So Simon went with Father; he was still in Tennessee with the army. We waited for Father to begin; we waited so long that we could tell from the sounds that Louvinia was almost through in the kitchen: so that I decided Father was waiting for Louvinia to finish and come in to hear too, so I said, 'How can you fight in mountains, Father?'

And that's what he was waiting for, though not in the way Ringo and I thought, because he said, 'You can't. You just have to. Now you boys run on to bed.'

We went up the stairs. But not all the way; we stopped and sat on the top step, just out of the light from the hall lamp, watching the door to the Office, listening; after a while Louvinia crossed the hall without looking up and entered the Office; we could hear Father and her:

'Is the trunk ready?'

'Yes, sir. Hit's ready.'

'Then tell Loosh to get the lantern and the shovels and wait in the kitchen for me.'

'Yes sir,' Louvinia said. She came out; she crossed the hall again without even looking up the stairs, who used to follow us up and stand in the bedroom door and scold at us until we were in bed – I in the bed itself, Ringo on the pallet beside it. But this time she not only didn't wonder where we were, she didn't even think about where we might not be.

'I knows what's in that trunk,' Ringo whispered. 'Hit's the silver. What you reckon –'

'Shhhh,' I said. We could hear Father's voice, talking to Granny. After a while Louvinia came back and crossed the hall again. We sat on the top step, listening to Father's voice telling Granny and Louvinia both.

'Vicksburg?' Ringo whispered. We were in the shadow; I couldn't see anything but his eyeballs. 'Vicksburg *fell*? Do he mean hit fell off in the River? With Ginrul Pemberton in hit too?'

'Shhhhh!' I said. We sat close together in the shadow, listening to Father. Perhaps it was the dark or perhaps we were the two moths, the two feathers again or perhaps there is a point at which credulity firmly and calmly and irrevocably declines, because suddenly Louvinia was standing over us, shaking us awake. She didn't even scold us. She followed us upstairs and stood in the door to the bedroom and she didn't even light the lamp; she couldn't have told whether or not we had undressed even if she had been paying enough attention to suspect that we had not. She may have been listening as Ringo and I were, to what we thought we heard, though I knew better, just as I knew that we had slept on the stairs for some time; I was telling myself, 'They have already carried it out, they are in the orchard now, digging.' Because there is the point at which credulity declines; somewhere between waking and sleeping I believed I saw or I dreamed that I did see the lantern in the orchard, under the apple trees. But I don't know whether I saw it or not, because then it was morning and it was raining and Father was gone.

3

He must have ridden off in the rain, which was still falling at breakfast and then at dinner-time too, so that it looked as if we wouldn't have to leave the house at all, until at last Granny put the sewing away and said, 'Very well. Get the cook book, Marengo.' Ringo got the cook book from the kitchen and he and I lay on our stomachs on the floor while Granny opened the book. 'What shall we read about today?' she said.

'Read about cake,' I said.

'Very well. What kind of cake?' Only she didn't need to say that because Ringo was already answering that before she spoke:

'Cokynut cake, Granny.' He said coconut cake every time because we never had been able to decide whether Ringo had ever tasted coconut cake or not. We had had some that Christmas before it started and Ringo had tried to remember whether they had had any of it in the kitchen or not, but he couldn't remember. Now and then I used to try to help him decide, get him to tell me how it tasted and what it looked like and sometimes he would almost decide to risk it before he would change his mind. Because he said that he would rather just maybe have tasted coconut cake without remembering it than to know for certain he had not; that if he were to describe the wrong kind of cake, he would never taste coconut cake as long as he lived.

'I reckon a little more won't hurt us,' Granny said.

The rain stopped in the middle of the afternoon; the sun was shining when I stepped out on to the back gallery, with Ringo already saying, 'Where we going?' behind me and still saying it after we passed the smokehouse where I could see the stable and the cabins: 'Where we going now?' Before we reached the stable Joby and Loosh came into sight beyond the pasture fence, bringing the mules up from the new pen. 'What we ghy do now?' Ringo said.

'Watch him,' I said.

'Watch him? Watch who?' I looked at Ringo. He was staring at me, his eyeballs white and quiet like last night. 'You talking about Loosh. Who tole us to watch him?'

'Nobody. I just know.'

'Bayard, did you dream hit?'

'Yes. Last night. It was Father and Louvinia. Father said to watch Loosh, because he knows.'

'Knows?' Ringo said. 'Knows what?' But he didn't need to ask that either; in the next breath he answered it himself, staring at me with his round quiet eyes, blinking a little: 'Yestiddy. Vicksburg. When he knocked it over. He knowed it then already. Like when he said Marse John wasn't at no Tennessee and sho enough Marse John wasn't. Go on; what else did the dream tole you?'

'That's all. To watch him. That he would know before we did. Father said that Louvinia would have to watch him too, that even if he was her son, she would have to be white a little while longer. Because if we watched him, we could tell by what he did when it was getting ready to happen.'

'When what was getting ready to happen?'

'I don't know.' Ringo breathed deep, once.

'Then hit's so,' he said. 'If somebody tole you, hit could be a lie. But if you dremp hit, hit can't be a lie case ain't nobody there to tole hit to you. So we got to watch him.'

We followed them when they put the mules to the wagon and went down beyond the pasture to where they had been cutting wood. We watched them for two days, hidden. We realized then what a close watch Louvinia had kept on us all the time. Sometimes while we were hidden watching Loosh and Joby load the wagon, we would hear her yelling at us, and we would have to sneak away and then run to let Louvinia find us coming from the other direction. Sometimes she would even meet us before we had time to circle, and Ringo hiding behind me then while she scolded at us: 'What devilment yawl into now? Yawl up to something. What is it?' But we didn't tell her, and we would follow her back to the kitchen while she scolded at us over her shoulder, and when she was inside the house we would move quietly until we were out of sight again, and then run back to hide and watch Loosh.

So we were outside of his and Philadelphy's cabin that night when he came out. We followed him down to the new pen and heard him catch the mule and ride away. We ran, but when we reached the road, too, we could only hear the mule loping, dying away. But we had come a good piece, because even Louvinia calling us sounded faint and small. We looked up the road in the starlight, after the mule. 'That's where Corinth is,' I said.

He didn't get back until after dark the next day. We stayed close to the house and watched the road by turns, to get Louvinia calmed down in case it would be late before he got back. It was late; she had followed us up to bed and we had slipped out again; we were just passing Joby's cabin when the door opened and Loosh kind of surged up out of the darkness right beside us. He was almost close enough for me to have touched him and he did not see us at all; all of a sudden he was just kind of hanging there against the lighted doorway like he had been cut out of tin in the act of running and was inside the cabin and the door shut black again almost before we knew what we had seen. And when we looked in the window he was standing in front of the fire, with his clothes torn and muddy where he had been hiding in swamps and bottoms from the Patrollers and with that look on his face again which resembled drunkenness but was not, as if he had not slept in a long time and did not want to sleep now, and Joby and Philadelphy leaning into the fire-light and looking at him and Philadelphy's mouth open too and the same look on her face. Then I saw Louvinia standing in the door. We had not heard her behind us yet there she was, with one hand on the door jamb, looking at Loosh, and again she didn't have on Father's old hat.

'You mean they gwinter free us all?' Philadelphy said.

'Yes,' Loosh said, loud, with his head flung back; he didn't even look at Joby when Joby said, 'Hush up, Loosh!' 'Yes!' Loosh said, 'Gin'ral Sherman gonter sweep the earth and the race gonter all be free!'

Then Louvinia crossed the floor in two steps and hit Loosh across the head hard with her flat hand. 'You black fool!' she said. 'Do you think there's enough Yankees in the whole world to whip the white folks?'

We ran to the house, we didn't wait for Louvinia; again we didn't know that she was behind us. We ran into the room where Granny was sitting beside the lamp with the Bible open on her lap and her neck arched to look at us across her spectacles. 'They're coming here!' I said. 'They're coming to set us free!'

'What?' she said.

'Loosh saw them! They're just down the road. It's General Sherman and he's going to make us all free!' And we watching her, waiting to see who she would send for to take down the musket – whether it would be Joby, because he was the oldest, or Loosh, because he had seen them and would know what to shoot at. Then she shouted, too, and her voice was strong and loud as Louvinia's:

'You Bayard Sartoris! Ain't you in bed yet? . . . Louvinia!' she shouted. Louvinia came in. 'Take these children up to bed, and if you hear another sound out of them tonight, you have my permission and my insistence, too, to whip them both.'

It didn't take us long to get to bed. But we couldn't talk, because Louvinia was going to bed on the cot in the hall. And Ringo was afraid to come up in the bed with me, so I got down on the pallet with him. 'We'll have to watch the road,' I said. Ringo whimpered.

'Look like hit haf to be us,' he said.

'Are you scared?'

'I ain't very,' he said. 'I just wish Marse John was here.'

'Well, he's not,' I said. 'It'll have to be us.'

We watched the road for two days, lying in the cedar copse. Now and then Louvinia hollered at us, but we told her where we were and that we were making another map, and besides, she could see the cedar copse from the kitchen. It was cool and shady there, and quiet, and Ringo slept most of the time, and I slept some too. I was dreaming – it was like I was looking at our place and suddenly the house and stable and cabins and trees and all were gone and I was looking at a place flat and empty as the sideboard, and it was growing darker and darker, and then all of a sudden I wasn't looking at it; I was there – a sort of frightened drove of little tiny figures moving on it; they were Father and Granny and Joby and Louvinia and Loosh and Philadelphy and Ringo and me – and then Ringo made a choked sound and I was looking at the road, and there in the middle of it, sitting on a bright bay horse and looking at the house through a field glass, was a Yankee.

For a long time we just lay there looking at him. I don't know what we had expected to see, but we knew what he was at once; I remember thinking, 'He looks just like a man,' and then Ringo and I were glaring at each other, and then we were crawling backwards down the hill without remembering when we started to crawl, and then we were running across the pasture towards the house without remembering when we got to our feet. We seemed to run forever, with our heads back and our fists clenched, before we reached the fence and fell over it and ran on into the house. Granny's chair was empty beside the table where her sewing lay.

'Quick!' I said. 'Shove it up here!' But Ringo didn't move; his eyes looked like door knobs while I dragged the chair up and climbed on to it and began to lift down the musket. It weighed about fifteen pounds, though it was not the weight so much as the length; when it came free, it and the chair and all went down with a tremendous clatter. We heard Granny sit up in her bed upstairs, and then we heard her voice: 'Who is it?'

'Quick! ' I said. 'Hurry!'

'I'm scared,' Ringo said.

'You Bayard! ' Granny said ... 'Louvinia! '

We held the musket between us like a log of wood. 'Do you want to be free?' I said. 'Do you want to be free?'

We carried it that way, like a log, one at each end, running. We ran through the grove towards the road and ducked down behind the honeysuckle just as the horse came around the curve. We didn't hear anything else, maybe because of our own breathing or maybe because we were not expecting to hear anything else. We didn't look again either; we were too busy cocking the musket. We had practised before, once or twice when Granny was not there and Joby would come in to examine it and change the cap on the nipple. Ringo held it up and I took the barrel in both hands, high, and drew myself up and shut my legs about it and slid down over the hammer until it clicked. That's what we were doing, we were too busy to look; the musket was already riding up across Ringo's back as he stooped, his hands on his knees and panting, 'Shoot the bastud! Shoot him! ' and then the sights came level, and as I shut my eyes I saw the man and the bright horse vanish in smoke. It sounded like thunder and it made as much smoke as a brush fire and I heard the horse scream, but I didn't see anything else; it was Ringo wailing, 'Great God, Bayard! Hit's the whole army! '

4

The house didn't seem to get any nearer; it just hung there in front of us, floating and increasing slowly in size, like something in a dream, and I could hear Ringo moaning behind me, and farther back still the shouts and the hoofs. But we reached the house at last; Louvinia was just inside the door, with Father's old hat on her head rag and her mouth open, but we didn't stop. We ran on into the room where Granny was standing beside the righted chair, her hand at her chest.

'We shot him, Granny! ' I cried. 'We shot the bastud! '

'What?' She looked at me, her face the same colour as her

hair almost, her spectacles shining against her hair above her forehead. 'Bayard Sartoris, what did you say?'

'We killed him, Granny! At the gate! Only there was the whole army, too, and we never saw them, and now they are coming.'

She sat down; she dropped into the chair, hard, her hand at her breast. But her voice was strong as ever:

'What's this? You, Marengo! What have you done?'

'We shot the bastud, Granny!' Ringo said. 'We kilt him!'

Then Louvinia was there, too, with her mouth still open, too, and her face like somebody had thrown ashes at her. Only it didn't need her face; we heard the hoofs jerking and sliding in the dirt, and one of them hollering, 'Get around to the back there, some of you!' and we looked up and saw them ride past the window – the blue coats and the guns. Then we heard the boots and spurs on the porch.

'Granny!' I said. 'Granny!' But it seemed like none of us could move at all; we just had to stand there looking at Granny with her hand at her breast and her face looking like she had died and her voice like she had died too:

'Louvinia! What is this? What are they trying to tell me?' That's how it happened – like when once the musket decided to go off, all that was to occur afterwards tried to rush into the sound of it all at once. I could still hear it, my ears were still ringing, so that Granny and Ringo and I all seemed to be talking far away. Then she said, 'Quick! Here!' and then Ringo and I were squatting with our knees under our chins, on either side of her against her legs, with the hard points of the chair rockers jammed into our backs and her skirts spread over us like a tent, and the heavy feet coming in and – Louvinia told us afterwards – the Yankee sergeant shaking the musket at Granny and saying,

'Come on, grandma! Where are they? We saw them run in here!'

We couldn't see; we just squatted in a kind of faint grey light and that smell of Granny that her clothes and bed and room all had, and Ringo's eyes looking like two plates of chocolate pudding and maybe both of us thinking how Granny had never whipped us for anything in our lives except lying, and that even when it wasn't even a told lie, but just keeping quiet, how she would whip us first and then make us kneel down and kneel down with us herself to ask the Lord to forgive us.

'You are mistaken,' she said. 'There are no children in this house nor on this place. There is no one here at all except my servant and myself and the people in the quarters.'

'You mean you deny ever having seen this gun before?'

'I do.' It was that quiet; she didn't move at all, sitting bolt upright and right on the edge of the chair, to keep her skirts spread over us. 'If you doubt me, you may search the house.'

'Don't you worry about that; I'm going to . . . Send some of the boys upstairs,' he said. 'If you find any locked doors, you know what to do. And tell them fellows out back to comb the barn and the cabins too.'

'You won't find any locked doors,' Granny said. 'At least, let me ask you –'

'Don't you ask anything, grandma. You set still. Better for you if you had done a little asking before you sent them little devils out with this gun.'

'Was there –' We could hear her voice die away and then speak again, like she was behind it with a switch, making it talk. 'Is he – it – the one who –'

'Dead? Hell, yes! Broke his back and we had to shoot him!'

'Had to – you had – shoot –' I didn't know horrified astonishment either, but Ringo and Granny and I were all three it.

'Yes, by God! Had to shoot him! The best horse in the whole army! The whole regiment betting on him for next Sunday –' He said some more, but we were not listening. We were not breathing either, glaring at each other in the grey gloom, and I was almost shouting, too, until Granny said it:

'Didn't – they didn't – Oh, Thank God! Thank God!'

'We didn't –' Ringo said.

'Hush!' I said. Because we didn't have to say it, it was like we had had to hold our breaths for a long time without knowing it, and that now we could let go and breathe again. Maybe that was why we never heard the other man, when he came in, at all; it was Louvinia that saw that, too – a colonel, with a bright short beard and hard bright grey eyes, who looked at Granny sitting

in the chair with her hand at her breast, and took off his hat.
Only he was talking to the sergeant.

'What's this?' he said. 'What's going on here, Harrison?'

'This is where they run to,' the sergeant said. 'I'm searching
the house.'

'Ah,' the colonel said. He didn't sound mad at all. He just
sounded cold and short and pleasant. 'By whose authority?'

'Well, somebody here fired on United States troops. I guess
this is authority enough.' We could just hear the sound; it was
Louvinia that told us how he shook the musket and banged the
butt on the floor.

'And killed one horse,' the colonel said.

'It was a United States horse. I heard the general say myself
that if he had enough horses, he wouldn't always care whether
there was anybody to ride them or not. And so here we are,
riding peaceful along the road, not bothering nobody yet, and
these two little devils – The best horse in the army; the whole
regiment betting – '

'Ah,' the colonel said. 'I see. Well? Have you found them?'

'We ain't yet. But these rebels are like rats when it comes to
hiding. She says that there ain't even any children here.'

'Ah,' said the colonel. And Louvinia said how he looked at
Granny now for the first time. She said how she could see his
eyes going from Granny's face down to where her skirt was
spread, and looking at her skirt for a whole minute and then
going back to her face. And that Granny gave him look for look
while she lied. 'Do I understand, madam, that there are no
children in or about this house?'

'There are none, sir,' Granny said.

Louvinia said he looked back at the sergeant. 'There are no
children here, sergeant. Evidently the shot came from somewhere else. You may call the men in and mount them.'

'But colonel, we saw them two kids run in here! All of us
saw them!'

'Didn't you just hear this lady say there are no children here?
Where are your ears, sergeant? Or do you really want the
artillery to overtake us, with a creek bottom not five miles
away to be got over?'

'Well, sir, you're colonel. But if it was me was colonel – '

'Then, doubtless, I should be Sergeant Harrison. In which case, I think I should be more concerned about getting another horse to protect my wager next Sunday than over a grandchildless old lady' – Louvinia said his eyes just kind of touched Granny now and flicked away – 'alone in a house which, in all probability – and for her pleasure and satisfaction, I am ashamed to say, I hope – I shall never see again. Mount your men and get along.'

We squatted there, not breathing, and heard them leave the house; we heard the sergeant calling the men up from the barn and we heard them ride away. But we did not move yet, because Granny's body had not relaxed at all, and so we knew that the colonel was still there, even before he spoke – the voice short, brisk, hard, with that something of laughing behind it: 'So you have no grandchildren. What a pity in a place like this which two boys would enjoy – sports, fishing, game to shoot at, perhaps the most exciting game of all, and none the less so for being, possibly, a little rare this near the house. And with a gun – a very dependable weapon, I see.' Louvinia said how the sergeant had set the musket in the corner and how the colonel looked at it now, and now we didn't breathe. 'Though I understand that this weapon does not belong to you. Which is just as well. Because if it were your weapon – which it is not – and you had two grandsons, or say a grandson and a Negro playfellow – which you have not – and if this were the first time – which it is not – someone next time might be seriously hurt. But what am I doing? Trying your patience by keeping you in that uncomfortable chair while I waste my time delivering a homily suitable only for a lady with grandchildren – or one grandchild and a Negro companion.' Now he was about to go, too: we could tell it even beneath the skirt; this time it was Granny herself:

'There is little of refreshment I can offer you, sir. But if a glass of cool milk after your ride –'

Only, for a long time he didn't answer at all; Louvinia said how he just looked at Granny with his hard bright eyes and that hard bright silence full of laughing. 'No, no,' he said. 'I thank you. You are taxing yourself beyond mere politeness and into sheer bravado.'

'Louvinia,' Granny said, 'conduct the gentleman to the dining-room and serve him with what we have.'

He was out of the room now, because Granny began to tremble now, trembling and trembling, but not relaxing yet; we could hear her panting now. And we breathed, too, now, looking at each other. 'We never killed him!' I whispered. 'We haven't killed anybody at all!' So it was Granny's body that told us again; only this time I could almost feel him looking at Granny's spread skirt where we crouched while he thanked her for the milk and told her his name and regiment.

'Perhaps it is just as well that you have no grandchildren,' he said. 'Since, doubtless, you wish to live in peace. I have three boys myself, you see. And I have not even had time to become a grandparent.' And now there wasn't any laughing behind his voice, and Louvinia said he was standing there in the door, with the brass bright on his dark blue and his hat in his hand and his bright beard and hair, looking at Granny without the laughing now: 'I won't apologize; fools cry out at wind or fire. But permit me to say and hope that you will never have anything worse than this to remember us by.' Then he was gone. We heard his spurs in the hall and on the porch, then the horse, dying away, ceasing, and then Granny let go. She went back into the chair with her hand at her breast and her eyes closed and the sweat on her face in big drops; all of a sudden I began to holler, 'Louvinia! Louvinia!' But she opened her eyes then and looked at me; they were looking at me when they opened. Then she looked at Ringo for a moment, but she looked back at me, panting.

'Bayard,' she said, 'what was that word you used?'

'Word?' I said. 'When, Granny?' Then I remembered; I didn't look at her, and she lying back in the chair, looking at me and panting.

'Don't repeat it. You cursed. You used obscene language, Bayard.'

I didn't look at her. I could see Ringo's feet too. 'Ringo did too,' I said. She didn't answer, but I could feel her looking at me; I said suddenly: 'And you told a lie. You said we were not here.'

'I know it,' she said. She moved. 'Help me up.' She got out

27

of the chair, holding to us. We didn't know what she was trying to do. We just stood there while she held to us and to the chair and let herself down to her knees beside it. It was Ringo that knelt first. Then I knelt, too, while she asked the Lord to forgive her for telling the lie. Then she rose; we didn't have time to help her. 'Go to the kitchen and get a pan of water and the soap,' she said. 'Get the new soap.'

5

It was late, as if time had slipped up on us while we were still caught, enmeshed by the sound of the musket and were too busy to notice it; the sun shone almost level into our faces while we stood at the edge of the back gallery, spitting, rinsing the soap from our mouths turn and turn about from the gourd dipper, spitting straight into the sun. For a while, just by breathing we could blow soap bubbles, but soon it was just the taste of the spitting. Then even that began to go away although the impulse to spit did not, while away to the north we could see the cloudbank, faint and blue and faraway at the base and touched with copper sun along the crest. When Father came home in the spring, we tried to understand about mountains. At last he pointed out the cloudbank to tell us what mountains looked like. So ever since then Ringo believed that the cloudbank was Tennessee.

'Yonder they,' he said, spitting. 'Yonder hit. Tennessee, where Marse John uses to fight um at. Looking mighty far, too.'

'Too far to go just to fight Yankees,' I said, spitting too. But it was gone now – the suds, the glassy weightless iridescent bubbles; even the taste of it.

Retreat

I

In the afternoon Loosh drove the wagon up beside the back gallery and took the mules out; by supper-time we had everything loaded into the wagon but the bedclothes we would sleep under that night. Then Granny went upstairs and when she came back down she had on her Sunday black silk and her hat, and there was colour in her face now and her eyes were bright.

'Is we gonter leave tonight?' Ringo said. 'I thought we wasn't going to start until in the morning.'

'We're not,' Granny said. 'But it's been three years now since I have started anywhere; I reckon the Lord will forgive me for getting ready one day ahead of time.' She turned (we were in the dining-room then, the table set with supper) to Louvinia. 'Tell Joby and Loosh to be ready with the lantern and the shovels as soon as they have finished eating.'

Louvinia had set the cornbread on the table and was going out when she stopped and looked at Granny. 'You mean you gonter take that heavy trunk all the way to Memphis with you? You gonter dig hit up from where hit been hid safe since last summer, and take hit all the way to Memphis?'

'Yes,' Granny said. 'I am following Colonel Sartoris' instructions as I believe he meant them.' She was eating; she didn't even look at Louvinia. Louvinia stood there in the pantry door, looking at the back of Granny's head.

'Whyn't you leave hit here where hit hid good and I can take care of hit? Who gonter find hit, even if they was to come here again? Hit's Marse John they done called the reward on; hit ain't no truck full of –'

'I have my reasons,' Granny said. 'You do what I told you.'

'All right. But how come you wanter dig hit up tonight when you ain't leaving until tomor –'

'You do what I said,' Granny said.

'Yessum,' Louvinia said. She went out. I looked at Granny eating, with her hat sitting on the exact top of her head, and

Ringo looking at me across the back of Granny's chair with his eyes rolling a little.

'Why not leave it hid?' I said. 'It'll be just that much more load on the wagon. Joby says that trunk will weigh a thousand pounds.'

'A thousand fiddlesticks!' Granny said. 'I don't care if it weighed ten thousand –' Louvinia came in.

'They be ready,' she said. 'I wish you'd tell me why you got to dig hit up tonight.'

Granny looked at her. 'I had a dream about it last night.'

'Oh,' Louvinia said. She and Ringo looked exactly alike, except that Louvinia's eyes were not rolling so much as his.

'I dreamed I was looking out my window, and a man walked into the orchard and went to where it is and stood there pointing at it,' Granny said. She looked at Louvinia. 'A black man.'

'A nigger?' Louvinia said.

'Yes.'

For a while Louvinia didn't say anything. Then she said, 'Did you know him?'

'Yes,' Granny said.

'Is you going to tell who hit was?'

'No,' Granny said.

Louvinia turned to Ringo. 'Gawn tell your pappy and Loosh to get the lantern and the shovels and come on up here.'

Joby and Loosh were in the kitchen. Joby was sitting behind the stove with a plate on his knees, eating. Loosh was sitting on the wood box, still, with the two shovels between his knees, but I didn't see him at first because of Ringo's shadow. The lamp was on the table, and I could see the shadow of Ringo's head bent over and his arm working back and forth, and Louvinia standing between us and the lamp, her hands on her hips and her elbows spread and her shadow filling the room. 'Clean that chimney good,' she said.

Joby carried the lantern, with Granny behind him, and then Loosh; I could see her bonnet and Loosh's head and the two shovel blades over his shoulder. Ringo was breathing behind me. 'Which un you reckon she drempt about?' he said.

'Why don't you ask her?' I said. We were in the orchard now.

'Hoo,' Ringo said. 'Me ask her? I bet if she stayed here

wouldn't no Yankee nor nothing else bother that trunk, nor Marse John neither, if he knowed hit.'

Then they stopped – Joby and Granny, and while Granny held the lantern at arm's length, Joby and Loosh dug the trunk up from where they had buried it that night last summer while Father was at home, while Louvinia stood in the door of the bedroom without even lighting the lamp while Ringo and I went to bed and later I either looked out or dreamed I looked out the window and saw (or dreamed I saw) the lantern. Then, with Granny in front and still carrying the lantern and with Ringo and I both helping to carry it, we returned towards the house. Before we reached the house Joby began to bear away towards where the loaded wagon stood.

'Take it into the house,' Granny said.

'We'll just load hit now and save having to handle hit again in the morning,' Joby said. 'Come on here, nigger,' he said to Loosh.

'Take it into the house,' Granny said. So, after a while, Joby moved on towards the house. We could hear him breathing now, saying 'Hah!' every few steps. Inside the kitchen he let his end down, hard.

'Hah!' he said. 'That's done, thank God.'

'Take it upstairs,' Granny said.

Joby turned and looked at her. He hadn't straightened up yet; he turned, half stooping, and looked at her. 'Which?' he said.

'Take it upstairs,' Granny said. 'I want it in my room.'

'You mean you gonter tote this thing all the way upstairs and then tote it back down tomorrow?'

'Somebody is,' Granny said. 'Are you going to help or are me and Bayard going to do it alone?'

Then Louvinia came in. She had already undressed. She looked tall as a ghost, in one dimension like a bolster case, taller than a bolster case in her nightgown; silent as a ghost on her bare feet which were the same colour as the shadow in which she stood so that she seemed to have no feet, the twin rows of her toenails lying weightless and faint and still as two rows of faintly soiled feathers on the floor about a foot below the hem of her nightgown as if they were not connected with her. She came

31

and shoved Joby aside and stooped to lift the trunk. 'Git away, nigger,' she said. Joby groaned, then he shoved Louvinia aside.

'Git away, woman,' he said. He lifted his end of the trunk, then he looked back at Loosh, who had never let his end down. 'If you gonter ride on hit, pick up your feet,' he said. We carried the trunk up to Granny's room, and Joby was setting it down again, until Granny made him and Loosh pull the bed out from the wall and slide the trunk in behind it; Ringo and I helped again. I don't believe it lacked much of weighing a thousand pounds.

'Now I want everybody to go right to bed, so we can get an early start tomorrow,' Granny said.

'That's you,' Joby said. 'Git everybody up at crack of day and it be noon 'fore we get started.'

'Nummine about that,' Louvinia said. 'You do like Miss Rosa tell you.' We went out; we left Granny there beside her bed now well away from the wall and in such an ungainly position that anyone would have known at once that something was concealed, even if the trunk which Ringo and I as well as Joby believed now to weigh at least a thousand pounds, could have been hidden. As it was, the bed merely underlined it. Then Granny shut the door behind us and then Ringo and I stopped dead in the hall and looked at one another. Since I could remember, there had never been a key to any door, inside or outside, about the house. Yet we had heard a key turn in the lock.

'I didn't know there was ere a key would fit hit,' Ringo said, 'let alone turn.'

'And that's some more of yawls' and Joby's business,' Louvinia said. She had not stopped; she was already reclining on her cot and as we looked towards her she was already in the act of drawing the quilt up over her face and head. 'Yawl get on to bed.'

We went on to our room and began to undress. The lamp was lighted and there was already laid out across two chairs our Sunday clothes which we too would put on tomorrow to go to Memphis in. 'Which un you reckin she dremp about?' Ringo said. But I didn't answer that; I knew that Ringo knew I didn't need to.

2

We put on our Sunday clothes by lamplight, we ate breakfast by it and listened to Louvinia above stairs as she removed from Granny's and my beds the linen we had slept under last night and rolled up Ringo's pallet and carried them downstairs; in the first beginning of day we went out to where Loosh and Joby had already put the mules into the wagon and where Joby stood in what he called his Sunday clothes too – the old frock coat, the napless beaver hat, of Father's. When Granny came out (still in the black silk and the bonnet as if she had slept in them, passed the night standing rigidly erect with her hand on the key which she had produced from we knew not where and locked her door for the first time Ringo and I knew of) with her shawl over her shoulders and carrying her parasol and the musket from the pegs over the mantel. She held out the musket to Joby. 'Here,' she said. Joby looked at it.

'We won't need hit,' he said.

'Put it in the wagon,' Granny said.

'Nome. We won't need nothing like that. We be in Memphis so quick won't nobody even have time to hear we on the road. I speck Marse John got the Yankees pretty well cleant out between here and Memphis anyway.'

This time Granny didn't say anything at all. She just stood there holding out the musket until after a while Joby took it and put it into the wagon. 'Now go get the trunk,' Granny said. Joby was still putting the musket into the wagon; he stopped, his head turned a little.

'Which?' he said. He turned a little more, still not looking at Granny standing on the steps and looking at him; he was not looking at any of us, not speaking to any of us in particular. 'Ain't I tole you?' he said.

'If anything ever came into your mind that you didn't tell to somebody inside of ten minutes, I don't remember it,' Granny said. 'But just what do you refer to now?'

'Nummine that,' Joby said. 'Come on here, Loosh. Bring that boy with you.' They passed Granny and went on. She didn't look at them; it was as if they had walked not only out of her sight but out of her mind. Evidently Joby thought they had. He and Granny were like that; they were like a man and a mare, a blooded mare, which takes just exactly so much from the man and the man knows the mare will take just so much and the man knows that when that point is reached, just what is going to happen. Then it does happen: the mare kicks him, not viciously but just enough, and the man knows it was going to happen and so he is glad then, it is over then, or he thinks it is over, so he lies or sits on the ground and cusses the mare a little because he thinks it is over, finished, and then the mare turns her head and nips him. That's how Joby and Granny were and Granny always beat him, not bad: just exactly enough, like now; he and Loosh were just about to go in the door and Granny still not even looking after them, when Joby said, 'I done tole um. An I reckin even you can't dispute hit.' Then Granny, without moving anything but her lips, still looking out beyond the waiting wagon as if we were not going anywhere and Joby didn't even exist, said,

'And put the bed back against the wall.' This time Joby didn't answer. He just stopped perfectly still, not even looking back at Granny, until Loosh said quietly,

'Gawn, pappy. Get on.' They went on; Granny and I stood at the end of the gallery and heard them drag the trunk out, then shove the bed back where it had been yesterday; we heard them on the stairs with the trunk – the slow, clumsy, coffin-sounding thumps. Then they came out on to the gallery.

'Go and help them,' Granny said without looking back. 'Remember, Joby is getting old.' We put the trunk into the wagon, along with the musket and the basket of food and the bedclothing, and got in ourselves – Granny on the seat beside Joby, the bonnet on the exact top of her head and the parasol raised even before the dew had begun to fall – and we drove away. Loosh had already disappeared, but Louvinia still stood at the end of the gallery with Father's old hat on top of her head rag. Then I stopped looking back, though I could feel Ringo beside me on the trunk turning every few yards, even after we were outside the gate and in the road to town. Then we came to the curve where we had seen the Yankee sergeant on the bright horse last summer.

'Hit gone now,' Ringo said. 'Good-bye, Sartoris; Memphis, how-dy-do!'

The sun was just rising when we came in sight of Jefferson; we passed a company of troops bivouacked in a pasture beside the road, eating breakfast. Their uniforms were not grey any more now; they were almost the colour of dead leaves and some of them didn't even have uniforms and one man waved a skillet at us and he had on a pair of blue Yankee pants with a yellow cavalry stripe like Father wore home last summer. 'Hey, Miss-ippi!' he shouted. 'Hooraw for Arkansaw!'

We left Granny at Mrs Compson's, to tell Mrs Compson good-bye and to ask her to drive out home now and then and look after the flowers. Then Ringo and I drove the wagon on to the store and we were just coming out with the sack of salt when Uncle Buck McCaslin came hobbling across the square, waving his stick and hollering, and behind him the captain of the company we had passed eating breakfast in the pasture. There were two of them; I mean, there were two McCaslins, Amodeus and Theophilus, twins, only everybody called them Buck and Buddy except themselves. They were bachelors, they had a big bottom-land plantation about fifteen miles from town. It had a big colonial house on it which their father had built and which people said was still one of the finest houses in the country when they inherited it. But it wasn't now, because Uncle Buck and Buddy didn't live in it. They never had lived in it since their father died. They lived in a two-room log house with about a dozen dogs, and they kept their niggers in the manor house. It didn't have any windows now and a child with a hairpin could unlock any lock in it, but every night when the niggers came up from the fields Uncle Buck or Uncle Buddy would drive them into the house and lock the door with a key almost as big as a horse pistol; probably they would still be locking the front door long after the last nigger had escaped out the back. And folks said that Uncle Buck and Uncle Buddy knew this and that the niggers knew they knew it, only it was like a game with rules – neither one of Uncle Buck or Uncle Buddy to peep round the corner of the house while the other was locking the door, none of the niggers to escape in such a way as to be seen even by unavoidable accident, nor to escape at any other time; they even said that the ones who couldn't get out while the door was being locked voluntarily considered themselves interdict until the next evening. Then they would hang the key on a nail beside the door and go back to their own little house full of dogs and eat supper and play head-and-head poker; and they said how no man in the state or on the river either would have dared to play with them even if they did not cheat, but that in the game as they played it between themselves, betting niggers and wagon-loads of cotton with one another on the turn of a single card, the Lord Himself might have held His own with one of them at a time, but that with both of them, even He would have lost His shirt.

There was more to Uncle Buck and Buddy than just that. Father said they were ahead of their time; he said they not only possessed, but put into practice, ideas about social relationship that maybe fifty years after they were both dead people would have a name for. These ideas were about land. They believed that land did not belong to people but that people belonged to land and that the earth would permit them to live on and out of it and use it only so long as they behaved and that if they did not behave right, it would shake them off just like a dog getting rid of fleas. They had some kind of a system of book-keeping which must have been even more involved than their betting score against one another, by which all their niggers were to be freed, not given freedom, but earning it, buying it not in money from Uncle Buck and Buddy, but in work from the plantation. Only there were others besides niggers, and this was the reason why Uncle Buck came hobbling across the square, shaking his stick at me and hollering, or at least why it was Uncle Buck who was hobbling and hollering and shaking the stick. One day Father said how they suddenly realized that if the county ever split up into private feuds either with votes or weapons, no family could contend with the McCaslins because all the other families would have only their cousins and kin to recruit from, while Uncle Buck and Buddy would already have an army. These were the dirt farmers, the people whom the niggers called 'white trash' – men who had owned no slaves and some of whom even lived worse than the slaves on big plantations. It

was another side of Uncle Buck's and Buddy's ideas about men
and land, which Father said people didn't have a name for yet,
by which Uncle Buck and Buddy had persuaded the white men
to pool their little patches of poor hill land along with the
niggers and the McCaslin plantation, promising them in return
nobody knew exactly what, except that their women and
children did have shoes, which not all of them had had before,
and a lot of them even went to school. Anyway, they (the white
men, the trash) looked on Uncle Buck and Buddy like Deity
Himself, so that when Father began to raise his first regiment to
take to Virginia and Uncle Buck and Buddy came to town to
enlist and the others decided they were too old (they were past
seventy), it looked for a while as if Father's regiment would
have to fight its first engagement right there in our pasture. At
first Uncle Buck and Buddy said they would form a company of
their own men in opposition to Father's. Then they realized that
this wouldn't stop Father, so then Uncle Buck and Buddy put
the thumbscrews on Father sure enough. They told Father that
if he did not let them go, the solid bloc of private soldier white
trash votes which they controlled would not only force Father
to call a special election of officers before the regiment left the
pasture, it would also demote Father from colonel to major or
maybe only a company commander. Father didn't mind what
they called him; colonel or corporal, it would have been all the
same to him, as long as they let him tell them what to do, and he
probably wouldn't have minded being demoted even to private
by God Himself; it was the idea that there could be latent within
the men he led the power, let alone the desire, to so affront him.
So they compromised; they agreed at last that one of the
McCaslins should be allowed to go. Father and Uncle Buck and
Buddy shook hands on it and they stuck to it; the following
summer after Second Manassas when the men did demote
Father, it was the McCaslin votes who stuck with and resigned
from the regiment along with Father and returned to Mississippi with him and formed his irregular cavalry. So one of them
was to go, and they decided themselves which one it would be;
they decided in the one possible manner in which the victor
could know that he had earned his right, the loser that he had
been conquered by a better man; Uncle Buddy looked at Uncle

37

Buck and said, 'All right, 'Philus, you old butter-fingered son of a bitch. Get out the cards.'

Father said it was fine, that there were people there who had never seen anything like it for cold and ruthless artistry. They played three hands of draw poker, the first two hands dealt in turn, the winner of the second hand to deal the third; they sat there (somebody had spread a blanket and the whole regiment watched) facing each other with the two old faces that did not look exactly alike so much as they looked exactly like something which after a while you remembered – the portrait of someone who had been dead a long time and that you knew just by looking at him he had been a preacher in some place like Massachusetts a hundred years ago; they sat there and called those face-down cards correctly without even looking at the backs of them apparently, so that it took sometimes eight and ten deals before the referees could be certain that neither of them knew exactly what was in the other's hand. And Uncle Buck lost: so that now Uncle Buddy was a sergeant in Tennant's brigade in Virginia and Uncle Buck was hobbling across the square, shaking his stick at me and hollering:

'By Godfrey, there he is! There's John Sartoris' boy!'

The captain came up and looked at me. 'I've heard of your father,' he said.

'Heard of him?' Uncle Buck shouted. By now people had begun to stop along the walk and listen to him, like they always did, not smiling so he could see it. 'Who ain't heard about him in this country? Get the Yankees to tell you about him sometime. By Godfrey, he raised the first damn regiment in Mississippi out of his own pocket, and took 'em to Ferginny and whipped Yankees right and left with 'em before he found out that what he had bought and paid for wasn't a regiment of soldiers but a congress of politicians and fools. Fools I say!' he shouted, shaking the stick at me and glaring with his watery fierce eyes like the eyes of an old hawk with the people along the street listening to him and smiling where he couldn't see it and the strange captain looking at him a little funny because he hadn't heard Uncle Buck before; and I kept on thinking about Louvinia standing there on the porch with Father's old hat on, and wishing that Uncle Buck would get through or hush so we could go on.

'Fools, I say!' he shouted. 'I don't care if some of you folks here do still claim kin with men that elected him colonel and followed him and Stonewall Jackson right up to spitting distance of Washington without hardly losing a man, and then next year turned around and voted him down to major and elected in his stead a damn feller that never even knowed which end of a gun done the shooting until John Sartoris showed him.' He quit shouting just as easy as he started but the shouting was right there, waiting to start again as soon as he found something else to shout about. 'I won't say God take care of you and your grandma on the road, boy, because by Godfrey you don't need God's nor nobody else's help; all you got to say is "I'm John Sartoris' boy; rabbits, hunt the canebrake" and then watch the blue-bellied sons of bitches fly.'

'Are they leaving, going away?' the captain said.

Then Uncle Buck began to shout again, going into the shouting easy, without even having to draw a breath: 'Leaving? Hell's skillet, who's going to take care of them around here? John Sartoris is a damn fool; they voted him out of his own private regiment in kindness, so he could come home and take care of his family, knowing that if he didn't wouldn't nobody around here be likely to. But that don't suit John Sartoris because John Sartoris is a damned confounded selfish coward, askeered to stay at home where the Yankees might get him. Yes, sir. So skeered that he has to raise him up another batch of men to protect him every time he gets within a hundred foot of a Yankee brigade. Scouring all up and down the country, finding Yankees to dodge; only if it had been me I would have took back to Ferginny and I'd have showed that new colonel what fighting looked like. But not John Sartoris. He's a coward and a fool. The best he can do is dodge and run away from Yankees until they have to put a price on his head, and now he's got to send his family out of the country; to Memphis where maybe the Union Army will take care of them, since it don't look like his own government and fellow citizens are going to.' He ran out of breath then, or out of words anyway, standing there with his tobacco-stained beard trembling and more

39

tobacco running on to it out of his mouth, and shaking his stick at me. So I lifted the reins; only the captain spoke; he was still watching me.

'How many men has your father got in his regiment?' he said.

'It's not a regiment, sir,' I said. 'He's got about fifty, I reckon.'

'Fifty?' the captain said. 'Fifty? We had a prisoner last week who said he had more than a thousand. He said that Colonel Sartoris didn't fight; he just stole horses.'

Uncle Buck had enough wind to laugh though. He sounded just like a hen, slapping his leg and holding to the wagon wheel like he was about to fall. 'That's it! That's John Sartoris! He gets the horses; any fool can step out and get a Yankee. These two damn boys here did that last summer – stepped down to the gate and brought back a whole regiment, and them just – How old are you, boy?'

'Fourteen,' I said.

'We ain't fourteen yit,' Ringo said. 'But we will be in September, if we live and nothing happens . . . I reckon Granny waiting on us, Bayard.'

Uncle Buck quit laughing. He stepped back. 'Git on,' he said. 'You got a long road.' I turned the wagon. 'You take care of your grandma, boy, or John Sartoris will skin you alive. And if he don't, I will!' When the wagon straightened out, he began to hobble along beside it. 'And when you see him, tell him I said to leave the horses go for a while and kill the blue-bellied sons of bitches. Kill them!'

'Yes, sir,' I said. We went on.

'Good thing for his mouth Granny ain't here,' Ringo said. She and Joby were waiting for us at the Compsons' gate. Joby had another basket with a napkin over it and a bottle neck sticking out and some rose cuttings. Then Ringo and I sat behind again, and Ringo turning to look back every few feet and saying, 'Good-bye, Jefferson. Memphis, how-dy-do!' And then we came to the top of the first hill and he looked back, quiet this time, and said, 'Suppose they don't never get done fighting.'

'All right,' I said. 'Suppose it.' I didn't look back.

At noon we stopped by a spring and Granny opened the

basket, and she took out the rose cuttings and handed them to Ringo.

'Dip the roots into the spring after you drink,' she said. They had earth still on the roots, in a cloth; when Ringo stooped down to the water, I watched him pinch off a little of the dirt and start to put it into his pocket. Then he looked up and saw me watching him, and he made like he was going to throw it away. But he didn't.

'I reckon I can save dirt if I want to,' he said.

'It's not Sartoris dirt though,' I said.

'I know hit,' he said.'Hit's closer than Memphis dirt though. Closer than what you got.'

'What'll you bet?' I said. He looked at me. 'What'll you swap?' I said. He looked at me.

'What you swap?' he said.

'You know,' I said. He reached into his pocket and brought out the buckle we had shot off the Yankee saddle when we shot the horse last summer. 'Gimmit here,' he said. So I took the snuff box from my pocket and emptied half the soil (it was more than Sartoris earth; it was Vicksburg too: the yelling was in it, the embattled, the iron-worn, the supremely invincible) into his hand. 'I know hit,' he said. 'Hit come from 'hind the smoke-house. You brung a lot of hit.'

'Yes,' I said. 'I brought enough to last.'

We soaked the cuttings every time we stopped and opened the basket, and there was some of the food left on the fourth day because at least once a day we stopped at houses on the road and ate with them, and on the second night we had supper and breakfast at the same house. But even then Granny would not come inside to sleep. She made her bed down in the wagon by the chest and Joby slept under the wagon with the gun beside him like when we camped on the road. Only it would not be exactly on the road but back in the woods a way; on the third night Granny was in the wagon and Joby and Ringo and I were under the wagon and some cavalry rode up and Granny said, 'Joby! the gun!' and somebody got down and took the gun away from Joby and they lit a pine knot and we saw the grey.

'Memphis?' the officer said. 'You can't get to Memphis.

There was a fight at Cockrum yesterday and the roads are full of Yankee patrols. How in hell – Excuse me, ma'am' (behind me Ringo said, 'Git the soap') ' – you ever got this far I don't see. If I were you, I wouldn't even try to go back, I'd stop at the first house I came to and stay there.'

'I reckon we'll go on,' Granny said, 'like John – Colonel Sartoris told us to. My sister lives in Memphis; we are going there.'

'Colonel Sartoris?' the officer said. 'Colonel Sartoris told you?'

'I'm his mother-in-law,' Granny said. 'This is his son.'

'Good Lord, ma'am. You can't go a step farther. Don't you know that if they captured you and this boy, they could almost force him to come in and surrender?'

Granny looked at him; she was sitting up in the wagon and her hat was on. 'My experience with Yankees has evidently been different from yours. I have no reason to believe that their officers – I suppose they still have officers among them – will bother a woman and two children. I thank you, but my son has directed us to go to Memphis. If there is any information about the roads which my driver should know, I will be obliged if you will instruct him.'

'Then let me give you an escort. Or better still, there is a house about a mile back; return there and wait. Colonel Sartoris was at Cockrum yesterday; by tomorrow night I believe I can find him and bring him to you.'

'Thank you,' Granny said. 'Wherever Colonel Sartoris is, he is doubtless busy with his own affairs. I think we will continue to Memphis as he instructed us.'

So they rode away and Joby came back under the wagon and put the musket between us; only, every time I turned over I rolled on it, so I made him move it and he tried to put it in the wagon with Granny, and she wouldn't let him, so he leaned it against a tree and we slept and ate breakfast and went on, with Ringo and Joby looking behind every tree we passed. 'You ain't going to find them behind a tree we have already passed,' I said. We didn't. We had passed where a house had burned, and then we were passing another house with an old white horse looking at us out of the stable door behind it, and then I saw six men running in the next field, and then we saw a dust cloud coming fast out of a lane that crossed the road.

Joby said, 'Them folks look like they trying to make the Yankees take they stock, running hit up and down the big road in broad daylight like that.'

They rode right out of the dust cloud without seeing us at all, crossing the road, and the first ten or twelve had already jumped the ditch with pistols in their hands, like when you run with a stick of stove wood balanced on your palm; and the last one came out of the dust with five men running and holding to stirrups, and us sitting there in the wagon with Joby holding the mules like they were sitting down on the whiffletrees and his mouth hanging open and his eyes like two eggs, and I had forgotten what the blue coats looked like.

It was fast – like that – all sweating horses with wild eyes, and men with wild faces full of yelling, and then Granny standing up in the wagon and beating the five men about their heads and shoulders with the umbrella while they unfastened the traces and cut the harness off the mules with pocket knives. They didn't say a word; they didn't even look at Granny while she was hitting them; they just took the mules out of the wagon, and then the two mules and the five men disappeared together in another cloud of dust, and the mules came out of the dust, soaring like hawks, with two men on them and two more just falling backwards over the mules' tails, and the fifth man already running, too, and the two that were on their backs in the road getting up with little scraps of cut leather sticking to them like a kind of black shavings in a sawmill. The three of them went off across the field after the mules, and then we heard the pistols away off like striking a handful of matches at one time, and Joby still sitting on the seat with his mouth still open and the ends of the cut reins in his hands, and Granny still standing in the wagon with the bent umbrella lifted and hollering at Ringo and me while we jumped out of the wagon and ran across the road.

'The stable,' I said. 'The stable!' While we were running up the hill toward the house, we could see our mules still galloping in the field, and we could see the three men running too. When we ran round the house, we could see the wagon, too, in the road, with Joby on the seat above the wagon tongue sticking straight out ahead, and Granny standing up and shaking the umbrella towards us, and even though I couldn't hear her I knew she was still shouting. Our mules had run into the woods, but the three men were still in the field and the old white horse was watching them, too, in the barn door; he never saw us until he snorted and jerked back and kicked over something behind him. It was a home-made shoeing box, and he was tied by a rope halter to the ladder to the loft, and there was even a pipe still burning on the ground.

We climbed on to the ladder and got on him, and when we came out of the barn we could still see the three men; but we had to stop while Ringo got down and opened the lot gate and got back on again, and so they were gone, too, by then. When we reached the woods, there was no sign of them and we couldn't hear anything, either, but the old horse's insides. We went on slower then, because the old horse wouldn't go fast again, anyway, and so we tried to listen, and so it was almost sunset when we came out into a road.

'Here where they went,' Ringo said. They were mule tracks. 'Tinney and Old Hundred's tracks bofe,' Ringo said. 'I know um anywhere. They done throwed them Yankees and heading back home.'

'Are you sure?' I said.

'Is I sure? You reckon I ain't followed them mules all my life and I can't tell they tracks when I see um? . . . Git up there, horse!'

We went on, but the old horse could not go very fast. After a while the moon came up, but Ringo still said he could see the tracks of our mules. So we went on, only now the old horse went even slower than ever because presently I caught Ringo and held him as he slipped off and then a little later Ringo caught and held me from slipping before I even knew that I had been asleep. We didn't know what time it was, we didn't care; we only heard after a time the slow hollow repercussion of wood beneath the horse's feet and we turned from the road and hitched the bridle to a sapling; we probably both crawled beneath the bridge already asleep; still sleeping, we doubtless continued to crawl. Because if we had not moved, they would

not have found us. I waked, still believing I dreamed of thunder.
It was light; even beneath the close weed-choked bridge Ringo
and I could sense the sun though not at once; for the time we
just sat there beneath the loud drumming, while the loose
planks of the bridge floor clattered and danced to the hooves;
we sat there for a moment staring at one another in the pale
jonquil-coloured light almost before we were awake. Perhaps
that was it, perhaps we were still asleep, were taken so suddenly
in slumber that we had not time to think of Yankees or anything else; we were out from beneath the bridge and already
running before we remembered having begun to move; I
looked back one time and (the road, the bridge, was five or six
feet higher than the earth beside it) it looked as if the whole rim
of the world was full of horses running along the sky. Then
everything ran together again as it had yesterday; even while
our legs still continued to run Ringo and I had dived like two
rabbits into a briar patch, feeling no thorn, and lay on our faces
in it while men shouted and horses crashed around us, then
hard hands dragged us, clawing and kicking and quite blind,
out of the thicket and on to our feet. Then sight returned – a
vacuum, an interval of amazing and dewy-breathed peace and
quiet while Ringo and I stood in a circle of mounted and dismounted men and horses. Then I recognized Jupiter standing
big and motionless and pale in the dawn as a mesmerized flame,
then Father was shaking me and shouting, 'Where's your
grandmother? Where's Miss Rosa?' and then Ringo, in a tone
of complete amazement: 'We done fergot Granny!'

'Forgot her?' Father shouted. 'You mean you ran away and
left her sitting there in that wagon in the middle of the road?'

'Lord, Marse John,' Ringo said. 'You know hit ain't no
Yankee gonter bother her if he know hit.'

Father swore. 'How far back did you leave her?'

'It was about three o'clock yesterday,' I said. 'We rode some
last night.'

Father turned to the others. 'Two of you boys take them up
behind you; we'll lead that horse.' Then he stopped and turned
back to us. 'Have you-all had anything to eat?'

'Eat?' Ringo said. 'My stomach think my throat been cut.'

Father took a pone of bread from his saddle bag and broke it

45

and gave it to us. 'Where did you get that horse?' he said.

After a while I said, 'We borrowed it.'

'Who from?' Father said.

After a while Ringo said, 'We ain't know. The man wasn't there.' One of the men laughed. Father looked at him quick, and he hushed. But just for a minute, because all of a sudden they all began to whoop and holler, and Father looking around at them and his face getting redder and redder.

'Don't you say a word, Colonel,' one of them said. 'Hooraw for Sartoris!'

We galloped back; it was not far; we came to the field where the men had run, and the house with the barn, and in the road we could still see the scraps of harness where they had cut it. But the wagon was gone. Father led the old horse up to the house himself and knocked on the porch floor with his pistol, and the door of the house was still open, but nobody came. We put the old horse back into the barn; the pipe was still on the ground by the overturned shoeing box. We came back to the road and Father sat Jupiter in the middle of the litter of harness scraps.

'You damn boys,' he said. 'You damn boys.'

When we went on now, we went slower; there were three men riding on ahead out of sight. In the afternoon, one of them came galloping back, and Father left Ringo and me with three others, and he and the rest rode on; it was almost sunset when they came back with their horses sweated a little and leading two new horses with the blue blankets under the saddles and U.S. burned on the horses' hips.

'I tole you they wasn't no Yankees gonter stop Granny,' Ringo said. 'I bet she in Memphis right now.'

'I hope for your sake she is,' Father said. He jerked his hand at the new horses. 'You and Bayard get on them.' Ringo went to one of the new horses. 'Wait,' Father said; 'the other one is yours.'

'You mean hit belong to me?' Ringo said.

'No,' Father said. 'You borrowed it.'

Then we all stopped and watched Ringo trying to get on his horse. The horse would stand perfectly still until he would feel Ringo's weight on the stirrup; then he would whirl completely around until his off side faced Ringo; the first time Ringo wound up lying on his back in the road.

'Get on him from that side,' Father said laughing.

Ringo looked at the horse and then at Father. 'Git up from the wrong side?' Ringo said. 'I knowed Yankees wasn't folks, but I never knowed before they horses ain't horses.'

'Get on up,' Father said. 'He's blind in his near eye.'

It got dark while we were still riding, and after a while I waked up with somebody holding me in the saddle, and we were stopped in some trees and there was a fire, but Ringo and I didn't even stay awake to eat, and then it was morning again and all of them were gone but Father and eleven more, but we didn't start off even then; we stayed there in the trees all day. 'What are we going to do now?' I said.

'I'm going to take you damn boys home, and then I've got to go to Memphis and find your grandmother,' Father said.

Just before dark we started; we watched Ringo trying to get on his horse from the nigh side for a while and then we went on. We rode until dawn and stopped again. This time we didn't build a fire; we didn't even unsaddle right away; we lay hidden in the woods, and then Father was waking me with his hand. It was after sunup and we lay there and listened to a column of Yankee infantry pass in the road, and then I slept again. It was noon when I waked. There was a fire now and a shote cooking over it, and we ate. 'We'll be home by midnight,' Father said.

Jupiter was rested. He didn't want the bridle for a while and then he didn't want Father to get on him, and even after we were started he still wanted to go; Father had to hold him back between Ringo and me. Ringo was on his right. 'You and Bayard better swap sides,' Father told Ringo, 'so your horse can see what's beside him.'

'He is going all right,' Ringo said. 'He like hit this way. Maybe because he can smell Jupiter another horse, and know Jupiter ain't fixing to get on him and ride.'

'All right,' Father said. 'Watch him though.' We went on. Mine and Ringo's horses could go pretty well, too; when I looked back, the others were a good piece behind, out of our dust. It wasn't far to sundown.

'I wish I knew your grandmother was all right,' Father said.

47

'Lord, Marse John,' Ringo said, 'is you still worrying about Granny? I been knowed her all my life; I ain't worried about her.'

Jupiter was fine to watch, with his head up and watching my horse and Ringo's, and boring a little and just beginning to drive a little. 'I'm going to let him go a little,' Father said. 'You and Ringo watch yourselves.' I thought Jupiter was gone then. He went out like a rocket, flattening a little. But I should have known that Father still held him, because I should have seen that he was still boring, but there was a snake fence along the road, and all of a sudden it began to blur, and then I realized that Father and Jupiter had not moved up at all, that it was all three of us flattening out up towards the crest of the hill where the road dipped like three swallows, and I was thinking, 'We're holding Jupiter. We're holding Jupiter,' when Father looked back, and I saw his eyes and his teeth in his beard, and I knew he still had Jupiter on the bit.

He said, 'Watch out, now,' and then Jupiter shot out from between us; he went out exactly like I have seen a hawk come out of a sage field and rise over a fence.

When they reached the crest of the hill, I could see sky under them and the tops of the trees beyond the hill like they were flying, sailing out into the air to drop down beyond the hill like the hawk; only they didn't. It was like Father stopped Jupiter in mid-air on top of the hill; I could see him standing in the stirrups and his arm up with his hat in it, and then Ringo and I were on them before we could even begin to think to pull, and Jupiter reined back on to his haunches, and then Father hit Ringo's horse across the blind eye with the hat and I saw Ringo's horse swerve and jump clean over the snake fence, and I heard Ringo hollering as I went on over the crest of the hill, with Father just behind me shooting his pistol and shouting, 'Surround them, boys! Don't let a man escape!'

There is a limit to what a child can accept, assimilate; not to what it can believe because a child can believe anything, given time, but to what it can accept, a limit in time, in the very time which nourishes the believing of the incredible. And I was still a child at that moment when Father's and my horses came over the hill and seemed to cease galloping and to float, hang sus-

pended rather in a dimension without time in it while Father
held my horse reined back with one hand and I heard Ringo's
half-blind beast crashing and blundering among the trees to
our right and Ringo yelling, and looked quietly down at the
scene beneath rather than before us – the dusk, the fire, the
creek running quiet and peaceful beneath a bridge, the muskets
all stacked carefully and neatly and nobody within fifty feet of
them and the men, the faces, the blue Yankee coats and pants
and boots, squatting about the fire with cups in their hands and
looking towards the crest of the hill with the same peaceful
expression on all their faces like so many dolls. Father's hat was
flung on to his head now, his teeth were showing and his eyes
were bright as a cat's.

'Lieutenant,' he said, loud, jerking my horse around, 'ride
back up the hill and close in with your troop on their right. Git!'
he whispered, slapping my horse across the rump with his hand.
'Make a fuss! Holler! See if you can keep up with Ringo – Boys,'
he said, while they still looked up at him; they hadn't even put
the cups down: 'Boys, I'm John Sartoris, and I reckon I've got
you.'

Ringo was the only difficult one to capture. The rest of
Father's men came piling over the hill, reining back, and I
reckon that for a minute their faces looked about like the
Yankees' faces did, and now and then I would quit thrashing
the bushes and I could hear Ringo on his side hollering and
moaning and hollering again, 'Marse John! You, Marse John!
You come here quick!' and hollering for me, calling Bayard
and Colonel and Marse John and Granny until it did sound like
a company at least, and then hollering at his horse again, and it
running back and forth. I reckon he had forgotten again and
was trying to get up on the nigh side again, until at last Father
said, 'All right, boys. You can come on in.'

It was almost dark then. They had built up the fire, and the
Yankees still sitting around it and Father and the others standing over them with their pistols while two of them were taking
the Yankees' pants and boots off. Ringo was still hollering off
in the trees. 'I reckon you better go and extricate Lieutenant
Marengo,' Father said. Only about that time Ringo's horse
came bursting out with his blind eye looking big as a plate and

still trotting in a circle with his knees up to his chin, and then Ringo came out. He looked wilder than the horse; he was already talking, he was saying, 'I'm gonter tell Granny on you, making my horse run – ' when he saw the Yankees. His mouth was already open, and he kind of squatted for a second, looking at them. Then he hollered, 'Look out! Ketch um! Ketch um, Marse John! They stole Old Hundred and Tinney!'

We all ate supper together – Father and us and the Yankees in their underclothes.

The officer talked to Father. He said, 'Colonel, I believe you have fooled us. I don't believe there's another man of you but what I see.'

'You might try to depart, and prove your point,' Father said.

'Depart? Like this? And have every darky and old woman between here and Memphis shooting at us for ghosts? . . . I suppose we can have our blankets to sleep in, can't we?'

'Certainly, Captain,' Father said. 'And with your permission, I shall now retire and leave you to set about that business.'

We went back into the darkness. We could see them about the fire spreading their blankets on the ground. 'What in the tarnation do you want with sixty prisoners, John?' one of Father's men said.

'I don't,' Father said. He looked at me and Ringo. 'You boys captured them. What do you want to do with them?'

'Shoot 'em,' Ringo said. 'This ain't the first time me and Bayard ever shot Yankees.'

'No,' Father said. 'I have a better plan than that. One that Joe Johnston will thank us for.' He turned to the others behind him. 'Have you got the muskets and ammunition?'

'Yes, Colonel,' somebody said.

'Grub, boots, clothes?'

'Everything but the blankets, Colonel.'

'We'll pick them up in the morning,' Father said. 'Now wait.'

We sat there in the dark. The Yankees were going to bed. One of them went to the fire and picked up a stick. Then he stopped. He didn't turn his head and we didn't hear anything or see anybody move. Then he put the stick down again and came back to his blanket. 'Wait,' Father whispered. After a while the fire had died down. 'Now listen,' Father whispered. So we sat there in the dark and listened to the Yankees sneaking off into the bushes in their underclothes. Once we heard a splash and somebody cursing, and then a sound like somebody had shut his hand over his mouth. Father didn't laugh out loud; he just sat there shaking.

'Look out for moccasins,' one of the others whispered behind us.

It must have taken them two hours to get done sneaking off into the bushes. Then Father said, 'Everybody get a blanket and let's go to bed.'

The sun was high when he waked us. 'Home for dinner,' he said. And so, after a while, we came to the creek; we passed the hole where Ringo and I learned to swim and we began to pass the fields, too, and we came to where Ringo and I hid last summer and saw the first Yankee we ever saw, and then we could see the house, too, and Ringo said, 'Sartoris, here we is; let them that want Memphis take hit and keep hit bofe.' Because we were looking at the house, it was like that day when we ran across the pasture and the house would not seem to get any nearer at all. We never saw the wagon at all; it was Father that saw it; it was coming up the road from Jefferson, with Granny sitting thin and straight on the seat with Mrs Compson's rose cuttings wrapped in a new piece of paper in her hand, and Joby yelling and lashing the strange horses, and Father stopping us at the gate with his hat raised while the wagon went in first. Granny didn't say a word. She just looked at Ringo and me, and went on, with us coming behind, and she didn't stop at the house. The wagon went on into the orchard and stopped by the hole where we had dug the trunk up, and still Granny didn't say a word; it was Father that got down and got into the wagon and took up one end of the trunk and said over his shoulder.

'Jump up here, boys.'

We buried the trunk again, and we walked behind the wagon to the house. We went into the back parlour, and Father put the musket back on to the pegs over the mantel, and Granny put down Mrs Compson's rose cuttings and took off her hat and looked at Ringo and me.

'Get the soap,' she said.

'We haven't cussed any,' I said. 'Ask Father.'

'They behaved all right, Miss Rosa,' Father said.

Granny looked at us. Then she came and put her hand on me and then on Ringo. 'Go upstairs –' she said.

'How did you and Joby manage to get those horses?' Father said.

Granny was looking at us. 'I borrowed them,' she said. – 'upstairs and take off your –'

'Who from?' Father said.

Granny looked at Father for a second, then back at us. 'I don't know. There was nobody there – take off your Sunday clothes,' she said.

It was hot the next day, so we only worked on the new pen until dinner and quit. It was even too hot for Ringo and me to ride our horses. Even at six o'clock it was still hot; the rosin was still cooking out of the front steps at six o'clock. Father was sitting in his shirt sleeves and his stockings, with his feet on the porch railing, and Ringo and I were sitting on the steps waiting for it to get cool enough to ride, when we saw them coming into the gate – about fifty of them, coming fast, and I remember how hot the blue coats looked. 'Father,' I said. 'Father!'

'Don't run,' Father said. 'Ringo, you go round the house and catch Jupiter. Bayard, you go through the house and tell Louvinia to have my boots and pistols at the back door; then you go and help Ringo. Don't run, now; walk.'

Louvinia was shelling peas in the kitchen. When she stood up, the bowl broke on the floor. 'Oh Lord,' she said. 'Oh Lord, Again?'

I ran then. Ringo was just coming round the corner of the house; we both ran. Jupiter was in his stall, eating; he slashed out at us, his feet banged against the wall right by my head twice, like pistols, before Ringo jumped down from the hay-rack on to his head. We got the bridle on him, but he wouldn't take the saddle. 'Get your horse and shove his blind side up!' I was hollering at Ringo when Father came in, running, with his boots in his hand, and we looked up the hill towards the house and saw one of them riding round the corner with a short carbine, carrying it one hand like a lamp.

'Get away,' Father said. He went up on to Jupiter's bare back like a bird, holding him for a moment and looking down at us. He didn't speak loud at all; he didn't even sound in a hurry. 'Take care of Granny,' he said. 'All right, Jupe. Let's go.'

Jupiter's head was pointing down the hallway towards the lattice half doors at the back; he went out again, out from between me and Ringo like he did yesterday, with Father already lifting him and I thinking, 'He can't jump through that little hole.' Jupiter took the doors on his chest, only they seemed to burst before he even touched them, and I saw him and Father again like they were flying in the air, with broken planks whirling and spinning around them when they went out of sight. And then the Yankee rode into the barn and saw us, and threw down with the carbine and shot at us point-blank with one hand, like it was a pistol, and said, 'Where'd he go, the rebel son of a bitch?'

Louvinia kept on trying to tell us about it while we were running and looking back at the smoke beginning to come out of the downstairs windows: 'Marse John setting on the porch and them Yankees riding through the flower beds and say, "Brother, we wanter know where the rebel John Sartoris live," and Marse John say, "Hey?" with his hand to his ear and his face look like he born loony like Unc Few Mitchell, and Yankee say, "Sartoris, John Sartoris," and Marse John say, "Which? Say which?" until he know Yankee stood about all he going to, and Marse John say, "Oh, John Sartoris. Whyn't you say so in the first place?" and Yankee cussing him for idiot fool, and Marse John say, "Hey? How's that?" and Yankee say, "Nothing! Nothing! Show me where John Sartoris is 'fore I put rope round your neck too!" and Marse John say, "Lemme git my shoes and I show you," and come into house limping, and then run down the hall at me and say, "Boots and pistols, Louvinia. Take care of Miss Rosa and the chillen," and I go to the door, but I just a nigger. Yankee say, "That woman's lying. I believe that man was Sartoris himself. Go look in the barn quick and see if that claybank stallion there"' – until Granny stopped and began to shake her.

'Hush!' Granny said. 'Hush! Can't you understand that Loosh has shown them where the silver is buried? Call Joby. Hurry!' She turned Louvinia towards the cabins and hit her exactly like Father turned my horse and hit him when we rode down the hill and into the Yankees, and then Granny turned to run back towards the house; only now it was Louvinia holding her and Granny trying to get away.

'Don't you go back there, Miss Rosa!' Louvinia said. 'Bayard, hold her; help me, Bayard! They'll kill her!'

'Let me go!' Granny said. 'Call Joby! Loosh has shown them where the silver is buried!' But we held her; she was strong and thin and light as a cat, but we held her. The smoke was boiling up now, and we could hear it or them – something – maybe all of them making one sound – the Yankees and the fire. And then I saw Loosh. He was coming up from his cabin with a bundle on his shoulder tied up in a bandanna and Philadelphy behind him, and his face looked like it had that night last summer when Ringo and I looked into the window and saw him after he came back from seeing the Yankees. Granny stopped fighting. She said, 'Loosh.'

He stopped and looked at her; he looked like he was asleep, like he didn't even see us or was seeing something we couldn't. But Philadelphy saw us; she cringed back behind him, looking at Granny. 'I tried to stop him, Miss Rosa,' she said. ''Fore God I tried.'

'Loosh,' Granny said, 'are you going too?'

'Yes,' Loosh said, 'I going. I done been freed; God's own angel proclamated me free and gonter general me to Jordan. I don't belong to John Sartoris now; I belongs to me and God.'

'But the silver belongs to John Sartoris,' Granny said. 'Who are you to give it away?'

'You ax me that?' Loosh said. 'Where John Sartoris? Whyn't he come and ax me that? Let God ax John Sartoris who the man name that give me to him. Let the man that buried me in the black dark ax that of the man what dug me free.' He wasn't looking at us; I don't think he could even see us. He went on.

''Fore God, Miss Rosa,' Philadelphy said, 'I tried to stop him. I done tried.'

'Don't go, Philadelphy,' Granny said. 'Don't you know he's leading you into misery and starvation?'

Philadelphy began to cry. 'I knows hit. I knows whut they tole him can't be true. But he my husband. I reckon I got to go with him.'

They went on. Louvinia had come back; she and Ringo were behind us. The smoke boiled up, yellow and slow, and turning copper-coloured in the sunset like dust; it was like dust from a road above the feet that made it, and then went on, boiling up slow and hanging and waiting to die away.

'The bastuds, Granny!' I said. 'The bastuds!'

Then we were all three saying it – Granny and me and Ringo, saying it together: 'The bastuds!' we cried. 'The bastuds! The bastuds!'

Raid

Granny wrote the note with pokeberry juice. 'Take it straight to Mrs Compson and come straight back,' she said. 'Don't you-all stop anywhere.'

'You mean we got to walk?' Ringo said. 'You gonter make us walk all them four miles to Jefferson and back, with them two horses standing in the lot doing nothing?'

'They are borrowed horses,' Granny said. 'I'm going to take care of them until I can return them.'

'I reckon you calls starting out to be gone you don't know where and you don't know how long taking care of – ' Ringo said.

'Do you want me to whup you?' Louvinia said.

'Nome,' Ringo said.

We walked to Jefferson and gave Mrs Compson the note, and got the hat and the parasol and the hand mirror, and walked back home. That afternoon we greased the wagon, and that night after supper Granny got the pokeberry juice again and wrote on a scrap of paper, 'Colonel Nathaniel G. Dick, —th Ohio Cavalry,' and folded it and pinned it inside her dress. 'Now I won't forget it,' she said.

'If you was to, I reckon these hellion boys can remind you,' Louvinia said. 'I reckon they ain't forgot him. Walking in that door just in time to keep them others from snatching them out from under your dress and nailing them to the barn door like two coon hides.'

'Yes,' Granny said. 'Now we'll go to bed.'

We lived in Joby's cabin then, with a red quilt nailed by one edge to a rafter and hanging down to make two rooms. Joby was waiting with the wagon when Granny came out with Mrs Compson's hat on, and got into the wagon and told Ringo to open the parasol and took up the reins. Then we all stopped and watched Joby stick something into the wagon beneath the quilts; it was the barrel and the iron parts of the musket that Ringo and I found in the ashes of the house.

'What's that?' Granny said. Joby didn't look at her.

'Maybe if they just seed the end of hit they mought think hit was the whole gun,' he said.

'Then what?' Granny said. Joby didn't look at anybody now.

'I was just doing what I could to help git the silver and the mules back,' he said.

Louvinia didn't say anything either. She and Granny just looked at Joby. After a while he took the musket barrel out of the wagon. Granny gathered up the reins.

'Take him with you,' Louvinia said. 'Leastways he can tend the horses.'

'No,' Granny said. 'Don't you see I have got about all I can look after now?'

'Then you stay here and lemme go,' Louvinia said. 'I'll git um back.'

'No,' Granny said. 'I'll be all right. I shall inquire until I find Colonel Dick, and then we will load the chest in the wagon and Loosh can lead the mules and we will come back home.'

Then Louvinia began to act just like Uncle Buck McCaslin did the morning we started to Memphis. She stood there holding to the wagon wheel and looked at Granny from under Father's old hat, and began to holler. 'Don't you waste no time on colonels or nothing!' she hollered. 'You tell them niggers to send Loosh to you, and you tell him to get that chest and them mules, and then you whup him!' The wagon was moving now; she had turned loose the wheel, and she walked along beside it, hollering at Granny: 'Take that pairsawl and wear hit out on him!'

'All right,' Granny said. The wagon went on; we passed the ash pile and the chimneys standing up out of it; Ringo and I found the insides of the big clock too. The sun was just coming up, shining back on the chimneys; I could still see Louvinia between them, standing in front of the cabin, shading her eyes with her hand to watch us. Joby was still standing behind her, holding the musket barrel. They had broke the gates clean off; and then we were in the road.

'Don't you want me to drive?' I said.

'I'll drive,' Granny said. 'These are borrowed horses.'

'Case even Yankee could look at um and tell they couldn't

keep up with even a walking army,' Ringo said. 'And I like to know how anybody can hurt this team lessen he ain't got strength enough to keep um from laying down in the road and getting run over with they own wagon.'

We drove until dark, and camped. By sunup we were on the road again. 'You better let me drive a while,' I said.

'I'll drive,' Granny said. 'I was the one who borrowed them.'

'You can tote this pairsawl a while, if you want something to do,' Ringo said. 'And give my arm a rest,' I took the parasol and he laid down in the wagon and put his hat over his eyes. 'Call me when we gitting nigh to Hawkhurst,' he said, 'So I can commence to look out for that railroad you tells about.'

That was how he travelled for the next six days – lying on his back in the wagon bed with his hat over his eyes, sleeping, or taking his turn holding the parasol over Granny and keeping me awake by talking of the railroad which he had never seen though I had seen it that Christmas we spent at Hawkhurst. That's how Ringo and I were. We were almost the same age, and Father always said that Ringo was a little smarter than I was, but that didn't count with us, any more than the difference in the colour of our skins counted. What counted was, what one of us had done or seen that the other had not, and ever since that Christmas I had been ahead of Ringo because I had seen a railroad, a locomotive. Only I know now it was more than that with Ringo, though neither of us were to see the proof of my belief for some time yet and we were not to recognize it as such even then. It was as if Ringo felt it too and that the railroad, the rushing locomotive which he hoped to see symbolized it – the motion, the impulse to move which had already seethed to a head among his people, darker than themselves, reasonless, following and seeking a delusion, a dream, a bright shape which they could not know since there was nothing in their heritage, nothing in the memory even of the old men to tell the others. 'This is what we will find'; he nor they could not have known what it was yet it was there – one of those impulses inexplicable yet invincible which appear among races of people at intervals and drive them to pick up and leave all security and familiarity of earth and home and start out, they don't know where, empty-handed, blind to everything but a hope and a doom.

We went on; we didn't go fast. Or maybe it seemed slow because we had got into a country where nobody seemed to live at all; all that day we didn't even see a house. I didn't ask and Granny didn't say; she just sat there under the parasol with Mrs Compson's hat on and the horses walking and even our own dust moving ahead of us; after a while even Ringo sat up and looked around.

'We on the wrong road,' he said. 'Ain't even nobody live here, let alone pass here.'

But after a while the hills stopped, the road ran out flat and straight; and all of a sudden Ringo hollered, 'Look out! Here they come again to git these uns!' We saw it, too, then – a cloud of dust away to the west, moving slow – too slow for men riding – and then the road we were on ran square into a big broad one running straight on into the east, as the railroad at Hawkhurst did when Granny and I were there that Christmas before the war; all of a sudden I remembered it.

'This is the road to Hawkhurst,' I said. But Ringo was not listening; he was looking at the dust, and the wagon stopped now with the horses' heads hanging and our dust overtaking us again and the big dust cloud coming slow up in the west.

'Can't you see um coming?' Ringo hollered. 'Git on away from here!'

'They ain't Yankees,' Granny said. 'The Yankees have already been here.' Then we saw it, too – a burned house like ours, three chimneys standing above a mound of ashes, and then we saw a white woman and a child looking at us from a cabin behind them. Granny looked at the dust cloud, then she looked at the empty broad road going on into the east. 'This is the way,' she said.

We went on. It seemed like we went slower than ever now, with the dust cloud behind us, and the burned houses and gins and thrown-down fences on either side, and the white women and children – we never saw a nigger at all – watching us from the nigger cabins where they lived now like we lived at home; we didn't stop. 'Poor folks,' Granny said. 'I wish we had enough to share with them.'

At sunset we drew off the road and camped; Ringo was looking back. 'Whatever hit is, we done went off and left hit,' he said. 'I don't see no dust.' We slept in the wagon this time, all three of us. I don't know what time it was, only that all of a sudden I was awake. Granny was already sitting up in the wagon. I could see her head against the branches and the stars. All of a sudden all three of us were sitting up in the wagon, listening. They were coming up the road. It sounded like about fifty of them; we could hear the feet hurrying, and a kind of panting murmur. It was not singing exactly; it was not that loud. It was just a sound, a breathing, a kind of gasping, murmuring chant and the feet whispering fast in the deep dust. I could hear women, too, and then all of a sudden I began to smell them.

'Niggers,' I whispered. 'Sh-h-h-h,' I whispered.

We couldn't see them and they did not see us; maybe they didn't even look, just walking fast in the dark with that panting, hurrying murmuring going on. And then the sun rose and we went on, too, along that big broad empty road between the burned houses and gins and fences. Before, it had been like passing through a country where nobody had ever lived; now it was like passing through one where everybody had died at the same moment. That night we waked up three times and sat up in the wagon in the dark and heard niggers pass in the road. The last time it was after dawn and we had already fed the horses. It was a big crowd of them this time, and they sounded like they were running, like they had to run to keep ahead of daylight. Then they were gone. Ringo and I had taken up the harness again when Granny said, 'Wait. Hush.' It was just one, we could hear her panting and sobbing, and then we heard another sound. Granny began to get down from the wagon. 'She fell,' she said. 'You-all hitch up and come on.'

When we turned into the road, the woman was kind of crouched beside it, holding something in her arms, and Granny standing beside her. It was a baby, a few months old; she held it like she thought maybe Granny was going to take it away from her. 'I been sick and I couldn't keep up,' she said. 'They went off and left me.'

'Is your husband with them?' Granny said.

'Yessum,' the woman said. 'They's all there.'

'Who do you belong to?' Granny said. Then she didn't

answer. She squatted there in the dust, crouched over the baby. 'If I give you something to eat, will you turn around and go back home?' Granny said. Still she didn't answer. She just squatted there. 'You see you can't keep up with them and they ain't going to wait for you,' Granny said. 'Do you want to die here in the road for buzzards to eat?' But she didn't even look at Granny; she just squatted there.

'Hit's Jordan we coming to,' she said. 'Jesus gonter see me that far.'

'Get in the wagon,' Granny said. She got in; she squatted again just like she had in the road, holding the baby and not looking at anything – just hunkered down and swaying on her hams as the wagon rocked and jolted. The sun was up; we went down a long hill and began to cross a creek bottom.

'I'll get out here,' she said. Granny stopped the wagon and she got out. There was nothing at all but the thick gum and cypress and thick underbrush still full of shadow.

'You go back home, girl,' Granny said. She just stood there. 'Hand me the basket,' Granny said. I handed it to her and she opened it and gave the woman a piece of bread and meat. We went on; we began to mount the hill. When I looked back she was still standing there, holding the baby and the bread and meat Granny had given her. She was not looking at us. 'Were the others there in that bottom?' Granny asked Ringo.

'Yessum,' Ringo said. 'She done found um. Reckon she gonter lose um again tonight though.'

We went on; we mounted the hill and crossed the crest of it. When I looked back this time the road was empty. That was the morning of the sixth day.

2

Late that afternoon we were descending again; we came around a curve in the late level shadows and our own quiet dust and I saw the graveyard on the knoll and the marble shaft at Uncle Dennison's grave; there was a dove somewhere in the cedars. Ringo was asleep again under his hat in the wagon bed but he waked as soon as I spoke, even though I didn't speak loud and didn't speak to him. 'There's Hawkhurst,' I said.

'Hawkhurst?' he said, sitting up. 'Where's that railroad?' on his knees now and looking for something which he would have to find in order to catch up with me and which he would have to recognize only through hearsay when he saw it: 'Where is it? Where?'

'You'll have to wait for it,' I said.

'Seem like I been waiting on hit all my life,' he said. 'I reckon you'll tell me next the Yankees done moved hit too.'

The sun was going down. Because suddenly I saw it shining level across the place where the house should have been and there was no house there. And I was not surprised; I remember that; I was just feeling sorry for Ringo, since (I was just fourteen then) if the house was gone, they would have taken the railroad too, since anybody would rather have a railroad than a house. We didn't stop; we just looked quietly at the same mound of ashes, the same four chimneys standing gaunt and blackened in the sun like the chimneys at home. When we reached the gate Cousin Denny was running down the drive towards us. He was ten; he ran up to the wagon with his eyes round and his mouth already open for hollering.

'Denny,' Granny said, 'do you know us?'

'Yessum,' Cousin Denny said. He looked at me, hollering, 'Come see –'

'Where's your mother?' Granny said.

'In Jingus' cabin,' Cousin Denny said; he didn't even look at Granny. 'They burnt the house!' he hollered. 'Come see what they done to the railroad!'

We ran, all three of us. Granny hollered something and I turned and put the parasol back into the wagon and hollered 'Yessum!' back at her, and ran on and caught up with Cousin Denny and Ringo in the road, and we ran on over the hill, and then it came in sight. When Granny and I were here before, Cousin Denny showed me the railroad, but he was so little then that Jingus had to carry him. It was the straightest thing I ever saw, running straight and empty and quiet through a long empty gash cut through the trees, and the ground, too, and full of sunlight like water in a river, only straighter than any river with the cross-ties cut off even and smooth and neat, and the light shining on the rails like on two spider threads, running straight on to where you couldn't even see that far. It looked clean and neat, like the yard behind Louvinia's cabin after she had swept it on Saturday morning, with those two little threads that didn't look strong enough for anything to run on running straight and fast and light, like they were getting up speed to jump clean off the world.

Jingus knew when the train would come; he held my hand and carried Cousin Denny, and we stood between the rails and he showed us where it would come from, and then he showed us where the shadow of a dead pine would come to a stob he had driven in the ground, and then you would hear the whistle. And we got back and watched the shadow, and then we heard it; it whistled and then it got louder and louder fast, and Jingus went to the track and took his hat off and held it out with his face turned back towards us and his mouth hollering, 'Watch now! Watch!' even after we couldn't hear him for the train; and then it passed. It came roaring up and went past; the river they had cut through the trees was all full of smoke and noise and sparks and jumping brass, and then empty again, and just Jingus' old hat bouncing and jumping along the empty track behind it like the hat was alive.

But this time what I saw was something that looked like piles of black straws heaped up every few yards, and we ran into the cut and we could see where they had dug the ties up and piled them and set them on fire. But Cousin Denny was still hollering, 'Come see what they done to the rails!' he said.

They were back in the trees; it looked like four or five men had taken each rail and tied it around a tree like you knot a green cornstalk around a wagon stake, and Ringo was hollering, too, now.

'What's them?' he hollered. 'What's them?'

'That's what it runs on!' Cousin Denny hollered.

'You mean hit have to come in here and run up and down around these here trees like a squirrel?' Ringo hollered. Then we all heard the horse at once; we just had time to look when Bobolink came up the road out of the trees and went across the branch in the wind. They said she was the best woman rider in the country.

'There's Dru!' Cousin Denny hollered. 'Come on! She's

been up to the river to see them niggers! Come on!' He and Ringo ran again. When I passed the chimneys, they were just running into the stable. Cousin Drusilla had already unsaddled Bobolink, and she was rubbing him down with a crokersack when I came in. Cousin Denny was still hollering. 'What did you see? What are they doing?'

'I'll tell about it at the house,' Cousin Drusilla said. Then she saw me. She was not tall; it was the way she stood and walked. She had on pants, like a man. She was the best woman rider in the country. When Granny and I were here that Christmas before the war and Gavin Breckbridge had just given Bobolink to her, they looked fine together; it didn't need Jingus to say that they were the finest-looking couple in Alabama or Mississippi either. But Gavin was killed at Shiloh and so they didn't marry. She came and put her hand on my shoulder.

'Hello,' she said.' Hello, John Sartoris.' She looked at Ringo. 'Is this Ringo?' she said.

'That's what they tells me,' Ringo said. 'What about that railroad?'

'How are you?' Cousin Drusilla said.

'I manages to stand hit,' Ringo said. 'What about that railroad?'

'I'll tell you about that tonight too,' Drusilla said.

'I'll finish Bobolink for you,' I said.

'Will you?' she said. She went to Bobolink's head. 'Will you stand for Cousin Bayard, lad?' she said. 'I'll see you-all at the house, then,' she said. She went out.

'Yawl sho must 'a' had this horse hid good when the Yankees come,' Ringo said.

'This horse?' Cousin Denny said. 'Ain't no damn Yankee going to fool with Dru's horse no more.' He didn't holler now, but pretty soon he began again: 'When they come to burn the house, Dru grabbed the pistol and run out here – she had on her Sunday dress – and them right behind her. She run in here and she jumped on Bobolink bareback, without even waiting for the bridle, and one of them right there in the door hollering, "Stop," and Dru said, "Get away, or I'll ride you down," and him hollering, "Stop! Stop!" with his pistol out too' – Cousin Denny was hollering good now – 'and Dru leaned down to

64

Bobolink's ear and said, "Kill him, Bob," and the Yankee jumped back just in time. The lot was full of them, too, and Dru stopped Bobolink and jumped down in her Sunday dress and put the pistol to Bobolink's ear and said, "I can't shoot you all, because I haven't enough bullets, and it wouldn't do any good anyway; but I won't need but one shot for the horse, and which shall it be?" So they burned the house and went away!' He was hollering good now, with Ringo staring at him so you could have raked Ringo's eyes off his face with a stick. 'Come on!' Cousin Denny hollered. 'Le's go hear about them niggers at the river!'

'I been having to hear about niggers all my life,' Ringo said. 'I got to hear about that railroad.'

When we reached the house Cousin Drusilla was already talking, telling Granny mostly, though it was not about the railroad. Her hair was cut short; it looked like Father's would when he would tell Granny about him and the men cutting each other's hair with a bayonet. She was sunburned and her hands were hard and scratched like a man's that works. She was telling Granny mostly: 'They began to pass in the road yonder while the house was still burning. We couldn't count them; men and women carrying children who couldn't walk and carrying old men and women who should have been at home waiting to die. They were singing, walking along the road singing, not even looking to either side. The dust didn't even settle for two days, because all that night they still passed; we sat up listening to them, and the next morning every few yards along the road would be the old ones who couldn't keep up any more, sitting or lying down and even crawling along, calling to the others to help them; and the others – the young strong ones – not stopping, not even looking at them. I don't think they even heard or saw them. "Going to Jordan," they told me. "Going to cross Jordan."'

'That was what Loosh said,' Granny said. 'That General Sherman was leading them all to Jordan.'

'Yes,' Cousin Drusilla said. 'The river. They have stopped there; it's like a river itself, dammed up. The Yankees have thrown out a brigade of cavalry to hold them back while they build the bridge to cross the infantry and artillery; they are all right until they get up there and see or smell the water. That's when they go mad. Not fighting; it's like they can't even see the horses shoving them back and the scabbards beating them; it's like they can't even see anything but the water and the other bank. They aren't angry, aren't fighting; just men, women and children singing and chanting and trying to get to that unfinished bridge or even down into the water itself, and the cavalry beating them back with sword scabbards. I don't know when they have eaten; nobody knows just how far some of them have come. They just pass here without food or anything, exactly as they rose up from whatever they were doing when the spirit or the voice or whatever it was told them to go. They stop during the day and rest in the woods; then, at night, they move again. We will hear them later – I'll wake you – marching on up the road until the cavalry stops them. There was an officer, a major, who finally took time to see I wasn't one of his men; he said, "Can't you do anything with them? Promise them anything to go back home?" But it was like they couldn't see me or hear me speaking; it was only that water and that bank on the other side. But you will see for yourself tomorrow, when we go back.'

'Drusilla,' Aunt Louise said, 'you're not going back tomorrow or any other time.'

'They are going to mine the bridge and blow it up when the army has crossed,' Cousin Drusilla said. 'Nobody knows what they will do then.'

'But we cannot be responsible,' Aunt Louise said. 'The Yankees brought it on themselves; let them pay the price.'

'Those Negroes are not Yankees, Mother,' Cousin Drusilla said. 'At least there will be one person there who is not a Yankee either.' She looked at Granny. 'Four, counting Bayard and Ringo.'

Aunt Louise looked at Granny. 'Rosa, you shan't go. I forbid it. Brother John will thank me to do so.'

'I reckon I will,' Granny said. 'I've got to get the silver anyway.'

'And the mules,' Ringo said; 'don't forget them. And don't yawl worry about Granny. She 'cide what she want and then she kneel down about ten seconds and tell God what she aim to do, and then she git up and do hit. And them that don't like hit can git outen the way or git trompled. But that railroad – '

'And now I reckon we better go to bed,' Granny said. But we didn't go to bed then. I had to hear about the railroad too; possibly it was more the need to keep even with Ringo (or even ahead of him, since I had seen the railroad when it was a railroad, which he had not) than a boy's affinity for smoke and fury and thunder and speed. We sat there in that slave cabin partitioned, like Louvinia's cabin at home, into two rooms by that suspended quilt beyond which Aunt Louisa and Granny were already in bed and where Cousin Denny should have been too except for the evening's dispensation he had received, listening too who did not need to hear it again since he had been there to see it when it happened; – we sat there, Ringo and I, listening to Cousin Drusilla and staring at each other with the same amazed and incredulous question: *Where could we have been at that moment? What could we have been doing, even a hundred miles away, not to have sensed, felt this, paused to look at one another, aghast and uplifted, while it was happening?* Because this, to us, was it. Ringo and I had seen Yankees; we had shot at one; we had crouched like two rats and heard Granny, unarmed and not even rising from her chair, rout a whole regiment of them from the library. And we had heard about battles and fighting and seen those who had taken part in them, not only in the person of Father when once or twice each year and without warning he would appear on the strong gaunt horse, arrived from beyond that cloudbank region which Ringo believed was Tennessee, but in the persons of other men who returned home with actual arms and legs missing. But that was it: men had lost arms and legs in sawmills; old men had been telling young men and boys about wars and fighting before they discovered how to write it down: and what petty precision to quibble about locations in space or in chronology, who to care or insist. *Now come, old man, tell the truth: did you see this? were you really there?* Because wars are wars: the same exploding powder when there was powder, the same thrust and parry of iron when there was not – one tale, one telling, the same as the next or the one before. So we knew a war existed; we had to believe that, just as we had to believe that the name for the sort of life we had led for the last three years was hardship and suffering. Yet we had no proof of it. In

fact, we had even less than no proof; we had had thrust into our
faces the very shabby and unavoidable obverse of proof, who
had seen Father (and the other men too) return home, afoot like
tramps or on crowbait horses, in faded and patched (and at times
obviously stolen) clothing, preceded by no flags nor drums and
followed not even by two men to keep step with one another,
in coats bearing no glitter of golden braid and with scabbards
in which no sword reposed, actually almost sneaking home to
spend two or three or seven days performing actions not only
without glory (ploughing land, repairing fences, killing meat
for the smoke house) and in which they had no skill but the very
necessity for which was the fruit of the absent occupations from
which, returning, they bore no proof – actions in the very
clumsy performance of which Father's whole presence seemed
(to us, Ringo and me) to emanate a kind of humility and
apology, as if he were saying, 'Believe me, boys; take my word
for it: there's more to it than this, no matter what it looks like.
I can't prove it, so you'll just have to believe me.' And then to
have it happen, where we could have been there to see it, and
were not: and this no poste and riposte of sweat-reeking
cavalry which all war-telling is full of, no galloping thunder of
guns to wheel up and unlimber and crash and crash into the
lurid grime-glare of their own demon-served inferno which
even children would recognize, no ragged lines of gaunt and
shrill-yelling infantry beneath a tattered flag which is a very
part of that child's make-believe. Because this was it: an interval, a space, in which the toad-squatting guns, the panting men
and the trembling horses paused, amphitheatric about the
embattled land, beneath the fading fury of the smoke and the
puny yelling, and permitted the sorry business which had
dragged on for three years now to be congealed into an irrevocable instant and put to an irrevocable gambit, not by two regiments or two batteries or even two generals, but by two
locomotives.

Cousin Drusilla told it while we sat there in the cabin which
smelled of new whitewash and even (still faintly) of Negroes.
She probably told us the reason for it (she must have known) –
what point of strategy, what desperate gamble not for preserva-
tion, since hope of that was gone, but at least for prolongation,

which it served. But that meant nothing to us. We didn't hear, we didn't even listen; we sat there in that cabin and waited and watched that railroad which no longer existed, which was now a few piles of charred ties among which green grass was already growing, a few threads of steel knotted and twisting about the trunks of trees and already annealing into the living bark, becoming one and indistinguishable with the jungle growth which had now accepted it, but which for us ran still pristine and intact and straight and narrow as the path to glory itself, as it ran for all of them who were there and saw when Ringo and I were not. Drusilla told about that too; 'Atlanta' and 'Chattanooga' were in it – the names, the beginning and the end – but they meant no more to us than they did to the other watchers – the black and the white, the old men, the children, the women who would not know for months yet if they were widows or childless or not – gathered, warned by grapevine, to see the momentary flash and glare of indomitable spirit starved by three years free of the impeding flesh. She told it (and now Ringo and I began to see it; we were there too) – the roundhouse in Atlanta where the engine waited; we were there, we were of them who (they must have) would slip into the roundhouse in the dark, to caress the wheels and pistons and iron flanks, to whisper to it in the darkness like lover to mistress or rider to horse, cajoling ruthlessly of her or it one supreme effort in return for making which she or it would receive annihilation (and who would not pay the price), cajoling, whispering, caressing her or it towards the one moment; we were of them – the old men, the children, the women – gathered to watch, drawn and warned by that grapevine of the oppressed, deprived of everything now save the will and the ability to deceive, turning inscrutable and impassive secret faces to the blue enemies who lived among them. Because they knew it was going to happen; Drusilla told that too: how they seemed to know somehow the very moment when the engine left Atlanta; it was as if the grey generals themselves had sent the word, had told them, 'You have suffered for three years; now we will give to you and your children a glimpse of that for which you have suffered and been denied.' Because that's all it was. I know that now. Even the successful passage of a hundred engines with trains of cars could not have changed the situation or its outcome; certainly not two free engines shrieking along a hundred yards apart up that drowsing solitude of track which had seen no smoke and heard no bell in more than a year. I don't think it was intended to do that. It was like a meeting between two iron knights of the old time, not for material gain but for principle – honour denied with honour, courage denied with courage – the deed done not for the end but for the sake of the doing – put to the ultimate test and proving nothing save the finality of death and the vanity of all endeavour. We saw it, we were there, as if Drusilla's voice had transported us to the wandering light-ray in space in which was still held the furious shadow – the brief section of track which existed inside the scope of a single pair of eyes and nowhere else, coming from nowhere and having, needing, no destination, the engine not coming into view but arrested in human sight in thunderous yet dreamy fury, lonely, inviolate and forlorn, wailing through its whistle precious steam which could have meant seconds at the instant of passing and miles at the end of its journey (and cheap at ten times this price) – the flaring and streaming smoke stack, the tossing bell, the starred Saint Andrew's cross nailed to the cab roof, the wheels and the flashing driving rods on which the brass fittings glinted like the golden spurs themselves – then gone, vanished. Only not gone or vanished either, so long as there should be defeated or the descendants of defeated to tell it or listen to the telling.

'The other one, the Yankee one, was right behind it,' Drusilla said. 'But they never caught it. Then the next day they came and tore the track up. They tore the track up so we couldn't do it again; they could tear the track up but they couldn't take back the fact that we had done it. They couldn't take that from us.'

We – Ringo and I – knew what she meant; we stood together just outside the door before Ringo went on to Miss Lena's cabin, where he was to sleep. 'I know what you thinking,' Ringo said. Father was right; he was smarter than me. 'But I heard good as you did. I heard every word you heard.'

'Only I saw the track before they tore it up. I saw where it was going to happen.'

'But you didn't know hit was fixing to happen when you seed the track. So nemmine that. I heard. And I reckon they ain't gonter git that away from me, neither.'

He went on, then I went back into the house and behind the quilt where Denny was already asleep on the pallet. Drusilla was not there only I didn't have time to wonder where she was because I was thinking how I probably wouldn't be able to go to sleep at all now though it was late. Then it was later still and Denny was shaking me and I remember how I thought then that he did not seem to need sleep either, that just by having been exposed for three or four seconds to war he had even at just ten acquired that quality which Father and the other men brought back from the front – the power to do without sleep and food both, needing only the opportunity to endure. 'Dru says to come on outdoors if you want to hear them passing,' he whispered.

She was outside the cabin; she hadn't undressed even. I could see her in the starlight – her short jagged hair and the man's shirt and pants. 'Hear them?' she said. We could hear it again, like we had in the wagon – the hurrying feet, the sound like they were singing in panting whispers, hurrying on past the gate and dying away up the road. 'That's the third tonight,' Cousin Drusilla said. 'Two passed while I was down at the gate. You were tired, and so I didn't wake you before.'

'I thought it was late,' I said. 'You haven't been to bed even. Have you?'

'No,' she said. 'I've quit sleeping.'

'Quit sleeping?' I said. 'Why?'

She looked at me. I was as tall as she was; we couldn't see each other's faces; it was just her head with the short jagged hair like she had cut it herself without bothering about a mirror, and her neck that had got thin and hard like her hands since Granny and I were here before. 'I'm keeping a dog quiet,' she said.

'A dog?' I said. 'I haven't seen any dog.'

'No. It's quiet now,' she said. 'It doesn't bother anybody any more now. I just have to show it the stick now and then.' She was looking at me. 'Why not stay awake now? Who wants to sleep now, with so much happening, so much to see? Living used to be dull, you see. Stupid. You lived in the same house your father was born in, and your father's sons and daughters had the sons and daughters of the same Negro slaves to nurse and coddle; and then you grew up and you fell in love with your acceptable young man, and in time you would marry him, in your mother's wedding gown, perhaps, and with the same silver for presents she had received; and then you settled down for ever more while you got children to feed and bathe and dress until they grew up, too; and then you and your husband died quietly and were buried together maybe on a summer afternoon just before suppertime. Stupid, you see. But now you can see for yourself how it is; it's fine now; you don't have to worry now about the house and the silver, because they get burned up and carried away; and you don't have to worry about the Negroes, because they tramp the roads all night waiting for a chance to drown in home-made Jordan; and you don't have to worry about getting children to bathe and feed and change, because the young men can ride away and get killed in the fine battles; and you don't even have to sleep alone, you don't even have to sleep at all; and so, all you have to do is show the stick to the dog now and then and say, "Thank God for nothing." You see? There. They've gone now. And you'd better get back to bed, so we can get an early start in the morning. It will take a long time to get through them.'

'You're not coming in now?' I said.

'Not yet,' she said. But we didn't move. And then she put her hand on my shoulder. 'Listen,' she said. 'When you go back home and see Uncle John, ask him to let me come there and ride with his troop. Tell him I can ride, and maybe I can learn to shoot. Will you?'

'Yes,' I said. 'I'll tell him you are not afraid too.'

'Aren't I?' she said. 'Hadn't thought about it. It doesn't matter anyway. Just tell him I can ride and that I don't get tired.' Her hand was on my shoulder; it felt thin and hard. 'Will you do that for me? Ask him to let me come, Bayard.'

'All right,' I said. Then I said, 'I hope he will let you.'

'So do I,' she said. 'Now you go back to bed. Good night.'

I went back to the pallet and then to sleep; again it was Denny shaking me awake; by sunup we were on the road again,

Drusilla on Bobolink riding beside the wagon. But not for long.

We began to see the dust almost at once and I even believed that I could already smell them though the distance between us did not appreciably decrease, since they were travelling almost as fast as we were. We never did overtake them, just as you do not overtake a tide. You just keep moving, then suddenly you know that the set is about you, beneath you, overtaking you, as if the slow and ruthless power, become aware of your presence at last, had dropped back a tentacle, a feeler, to gather you in and sweep you remorselessly on. Singly, in couples, in groups and families they began to appear from the woods, ahead of us, alongside of us and behind; they covered and hid from sight the road exactly as an infiltration of flood water would have, hiding the road from sight and then the very wheels of the wagon in which we rode, our two horses as well as Bobolink breasting slowly on, enclosed by a mass of heads and shoulders – men and women carrying babies and dragging older children by the hand, old men and women on improvised sticks and crutches, and very old ones sitting beside the road and even calling to us when we passed; there was one old woman who even walked along beside the wagon, holding to the bed and begging Granny to at least let her see the river before she died.

But mostly they did not look at us. We might not have even been there. We did not even ask them to let us through because we could look at their faces and know they couldn't have heard us. They were not singing yet, they were just hurrying, while our horses pushed slow through them, among the blank eyes not looking at anything out of faces caked with dust and sweat, breasting slowly and terrifically through them as if we were driving in midstream up a creek full of floating logs and the dust and the smell of them everywhere and Granny in Mrs Compson's hat sitting bolt upright under the parasol which Ringo held and looking sicker and sicker, and it already afternoon though we didn't know it any more than we knew how many miles we had come. Then all of a sudden we reached the river, where the cavalry was holding them back from the bridge. It was just a sound at first, like wind, like it might be in the dust itself. We didn't even know what it was until we saw Drusilla holding Bobolink reined back, her face turned towards us wan and small above the dust and her mouth open and crying thinly: 'Look out, Aunt Rosa! Oh, look out!'

It was like we all heard it at the same time – we in the wagon and on the horse, they all around us in the sweat-caking dust. They made a kind of long wailing sound, and then I felt the whole wagon lift clear of the ground and begin to rush forward. I saw our old rib-gaunted horses standing on their hind feet one minute and then turned sideways in the traces the next, and Drusilla leaning forward a little and taut as a pistol hammer holding Bobolink, and I saw men and women and children going down under the horses and we could feel the wagon going over them and we could hear them screaming. And we couldn't stop any more than if the earth had tilted up and was sliding us all down towards the river.

It went fast, like that, like it did every time anybody named Sartoris or Millard came within sight, hearing or smell of Yankees, as if Yankees were not a people nor a belief nor even a form of behaviour, but instead were a kind of gully, precipice, into which Granny and Ringo and I were sucked pell-mell every time we got close to them. It was sunset; now there was a high bright rosy glow quiet beyond the trees and shining on the river, and now we could see it plain – the tide of niggers dammed back from the entrance to the bridge by a detachment of cavalry, the river like a sheet of rosy glass beneath the delicate arch of the bridge which the tail of the Yankee column was just crossing. They were in silhouette, running tiny and high above the placid water; I remember the horses' and mules' heads all mixed up among the bayonets, and the barrels of cannon tilted up and kind of rushing slow across the high peaceful rosy air like splitcane clothes-pins being jerked along a clothesline, and the singing everywhere up and down the river bank, with the voices of the women coming out of it thin and high: 'Glory! Glory! Hallelujah!'

They were fighting now, the horses rearing and shoving against them, the troopers beating at them with their scabbards, holding them clear of the bridge while the last of the infantry began to cross; all of a sudden there was an officer beside the wagon, holding his scabbarded sword by the little end like a stick and hanging on to the wagon and screaming at us. I don't know where he came from, how he ever got to us, but there he was with his little white face with a stubble of beard and a long streak of blood on it, bareheaded and with his mouth open. 'Get back!' he shrieked. 'Get back! We're going to blow the bridge!' screaming right into Granny's face while she shouted back at him with Mrs Compson's hat knocked to one side of her head and hers and the Yankee's faces not a yard apart:

'I want my silver! I'm John Sartoris' mother-in-law! Send Colonel Dick to me!' Then the Yankee officer was gone, right in the middle of shouting and beating at the nigger heads with his sabre, with his little bloody shrieking face and all. I don't know where he went any more than I know where he came from: he just vanished still holding on to the wagon and flailing about him with the sabre, and then Cousin Drusilla was there on Bobolink; she had our nigh horse by the head-stall and was trying to turn the wagon sideways. I started to jump down to help. 'Stay in the wagon,' she said. She didn't shout; she just said it. 'Take the lines and turn them.' When we got the wagon turned sideways we stopped. And then for a minute I thought we were going backwards, until I saw it was the niggers. Then I saw that the cavalry had broken; I saw the whole mob of it – horses and men and sabres and niggers – rolling on towards the end of the bridge like when a dam breaks, for about ten clear seconds behind the last of the infantry. And then the bridge vanished. I was looking right at it; I could see the clear gap between the infantry and the wave of niggers and cavalry, with a little empty thread of bridge joining them together in the air above the water, and then there was a bright glare and I felt my insides suck and a clap of wind hit me on the back of the head. I didn't hear anything at all. I just sat there in the wagon with a funny buzzing in my ears and a funny taste in my mouth, and watched little toy men and horses and pieces of plank floating along in the air above the water. But I didn't hear anything at all; I couldn't even hear Cousin Drusilla. She was right beside the wagon now, leaning towards us, her mouth urgent and wide and no sound coming out of it at all.

'What?' I said.

'Stay in the wagon!'

'I can't hear you!' I said. That's what I said, that's what I was thinking; I didn't realize even then that the wagon was moving again. But then I did; it was like the whole long bank of the river had turned and risen under us and was rushing us down towards the water, we sitting in the wagon and rushing down towards the water on another river of faces that couldn't see or hear either. Cousin Drusilla had the nigh horse by the bridle again, and I dragged at them, too, and Granny was standing up in the wagon and beating at the faces with Mrs Compson's parasol, and then the whole rotten bridle came off in Cousin Drusilla's hand.

'Get away!' I said. 'The wagon will float!'

'Yes,' she said, 'it will float. Just stay in it. Watch Aunt Rosa and Ringo.'

'Yes,' I said. Then she was gone. We passed her; turned, and holding Bobolink like a rock again and leaning down talking to him and patting his cheek, she was gone. Then maybe the bank did cave. I don't know. I didn't even know we were in the river. It was just like the earth had fallen out from under the wagon and the faces and all, and we all rushed down slow, with the faces looking up and their eyes blind and their mouths open and their arms held up. High up in the air across the river I saw a cliff and a big fire on it running fast sideways; and then all of a sudden the wagon was moving fast sideways, and then a dead horse came shining up from out of the yelling faces and went down slow again, exactly like a fish feeding, with, hanging over his rump by one stirrup, a man in a black uniform, and then I realized that the uniform was blue, only it was wet. They were screaming then, and now I could feel the wagon bed tilt and slide as they caught at it. Granny was kneeling beside me now, hitting at the screaming faces with Mrs Compson's parasol. Behind us they were still marching down the bank and into the river, singing.

3

A Yankee patrol helped Ringo and me cut the drowned horses out of the harness and drag the wagon ashore. We sprinkled water on Granny until she came to, and they rigged harness with ropes and hitched up two of their horses. There was a road on top of the bluff, and then we could see the fires along the bank. They were still singing on the other side of the river, but it was quieter now. But there were patrols still riding up and down the cliff on this side, and squads of infantry down at the water where the fires were. Then we began to pass between rows of tents, with Granny lying against me, and I could see her face then; it was white and still, and her eyes were shut. She looked old and tired; I hadn't realized how old and little she was. Then we began to pass big fires, with niggers in wet clothes crouching around them and soldiers going among them passing out food; then we came to a broad street, and stopped before a tent with a sentry at the door and a light inside. The soldiers looked at Granny.

'We better take her to the hospital,' one of them said.

Granny opened her eyes; she tried to sit up. 'No,' she said. 'Just take me to Colonel Dick. I will be all right then.'

They carried her into the tent and put her in a chair. She hadn't moved; she was sitting there with her eyes closed and a strand of wet hair sticking to her face when Colonel Dick came in. I had never seen him before – only heard his voice while Ringo and I were squatting under Granny's skirt and holding our breath – but I knew him at once, with his bright beard and his hard bright eyes, stooping over Granny and saying, 'Damn this war. Damn it. Damn it.'

'They took the silver and the darkies and the mules,' Granny said. 'I have come to get them.'

'Have them you shall,' he said, 'if they are anywhere in this corps. I'll see the general myself.' He was looking at Ringo and me now. 'Ha!' he said. 'I believe we have met before also.' Then he was gone again.

It was hot in the tent, and quiet, with three flies swirling around the lantern, and outside the sound of the army like wind far away. Ringo was already asleep, sitting on the ground with his head on his knees, and I wasn't much better, because all of a sudden Colonel Dick was back and there was an orderly writing at the table, and Granny sitting again with her eyes closed in her white face.

'Maybe you can describe them,' Colonel Dick said to me.

'I will do it,' Granny said. She didn't open her eyes. 'The chest of silver tied with hemp rope. The rope was new. Two darkies, Loosh and Philadelphy. The mules, Old Hundred and Tinney.'

Colonel Dick turned and watched the orderly writing. 'Have you got that?' he said.

The orderly looked at what he had written. 'I guess the general will be glad to give them twice the silver and mules just for taking that many niggers,' he said.

'Now I'll go see the general,' Colonel Dick said.

Then we were moving again. I don't know how long it had been, because they had to wake me and Ringo both; we were in the wagon again, with two Army horses pulling it on down the long broad street, and there was another officer with us and Colonel Dick was gone. We came to a pile of chests and boxes that looked higher than a mountain. There was a rope pen behind it full of mules and then, standing to one side and waiting there, was what looked like a thousand niggers, men, women and children, with their wet clothes dried on them. And now it began to go fast again; there was Granny in the wagon with her eyes wide open now and the lieutenant reading from the paper and the soldiers jerking chests and trunks out of the pile. 'Ten chests tied with hemp rope,' the lieutenant read. 'Get them? . . . A hundred and ten mules. It says from Philadelphia – that's in Mississippi. Get these Mississippi mules. They are to have rope and halters.'

'We ain't got a hundred and ten Mississippi mules,' the sergeant said.

'Get what we have got. Hurry.' He turned to Granny. 'And there are your niggers, madam.'

Granny was looking at him with her eyes wide as Ringo's. She was drawn back a little, with her hand at her chest. 'But they're not – they ain't – ' she said.

'They ain't all yours?' the lieutenant said. 'I know it. The general said to give you another hundred with his compliments.'

'But that ain't – We didn't – ' Granny said.

'She wants the house back, too,' the sergeant said. 'We ain't got any houses, grandma,' he said. 'You'll just have to make out with trunks and niggers and mules. You wouldn't have room for it on the wagon, anyway.'

We sat there while they loaded the ten trunks into the wagon. It just did hold them all. They got another set of trees and harness, and hitched four mules to it. 'One of you darkies that can handle two span come here,' the lieutenant said. One of the niggers came and got on the seat with Granny; none of us had ever seen him before. Behind us they were leading the mules out of the pen.

'You want to let some of the women ride?' the lieutenant said.

'Yes,' Granny whispered.

'Come on,' the lieutenant said. 'Just one to a mule, now.' Then he handed me the paper. 'Here you are. There's a ford about twenty miles up the river; you can cross there. You better get on away from here before any more of these niggers decide to go with you.'

We rode until daylight, with the ten chests in the wagon and the mules and our army of niggers behind. Granny had not moved, sitting there beside the strange nigger with Mrs Compson's hat on and the parasol in her hand. But she was not asleep, because when it got light enough to see, she said, 'Stop the wagon.' The wagon stopped. She turned and looked at me. 'Let me see that paper,' she said.

We opened the paper and looked at it, at the neat writing:

> Field Headquarters,
> —th Army Corps,
> Department of Tennessee,
> August 14, 1863.

To all Brigade, Regimental and Other Commanders: You will see that bearer is repossessed in full of the following property, to wit: Ten (10) chests tied with hemp rope and containing silver. One hundred ten (110) mules captured loose near Philadelphia in Mississippi. One hundred ten (110) Negroes of both sexes belonging to and having strayed from the same locality.

You will further see that bearer is supplied with necessary food and forage to expedite his passage to his destination.

By Order of the General Commanding.

We looked at one another in the grey light. 'I reckon you gonter take um back now,' Ringo said.

Granny looked at me. 'We can get food and fodder too,' I said.

'Yes,' Granny said. 'I tried to tell them better. You and Ringo heard me. It's the hand of God.'

We stopped and slept until noon. That afternoon we came to the ford. We had already started down the bluff when we saw the troop of cavalry camped there. It was too late to stop.

'They done found hit out and headed us off,' Ringo said. It was too late; already an officer and two men were riding towards us.

'I will tell them the truth,' Granny said. 'We have done nothing.' She sat there, drawn back a little again, with her hand already raised and holding the paper out in the other when they rode up. The officer was a heavy-built man with a red face; he looked at us and took the paper and read it and began to swear. He sat there on his horse swearing while we watched him.

'How many do you lack?' he said.

'How many do I what?' Granny said.

'Mules!' the officer shouted. 'Mules! Mules! Do I look like I had any chests of silver or niggers tied with hemp rope?'

'Do we –' Granny said, with her hand to her chest, looking at him; I reckon it was Ringo that knew first what he meant.

'We like fifty,' Ringo said.

'Fifty, hey?' the officer said. He cursed again; he turned to one of the men behind him and cursed him now. 'Count 'em!' he said. 'Do you think I'm going to take their word for it?'

The man counted the mules: we didn't move; I don't think we even breathed hardly. 'Sixty-three,' the man said.

The officer looked at us. 'Sixty-three from a hundred and ten leaves forty-seven,' he said. He cursed. 'Get forty-seven mules! Hurry!' He looked at us again. 'Think you can beat me out of three mules, hey?'

'Forty-seven will do,' Ringo said. 'Only I reckon maybe we better eat something, like the paper mention.'

We crossed the ford. We didn't stop; we went on as soon as they brought up the other mules, and some more of the women got on them. We went on. It was after sundown then, but we didn't stop.

'Hah!' Ringo said. 'Whose hand was that?'

We went on until midnight before we stopped. This time it was Ringo that Granny was looking at. 'Ringo,' she said.

'I never said nothing the paper never said,' Ringo said. 'Hit was the one that said it; hit wasn't me. All I done was to told him how much the hundred and ten liked; I never said we liked that many. 'Sides, hit ain't no use in praying about hit now; ain't no telling what we gonter run into 'fore we gits home. The main thing now is, whut we gonter do with all these niggers.'

'Yes,' Granny said. We cooked and ate the food the cavalry officer gave us; then Granny told all the niggers that lived in Alabama to come forward. It was about half of them. 'I suppose you all want to cross some more rivers and run after the Yankee Army, don't you?' Granny said. They stood there, moving their feet in the dust. 'What? Don't any of you want to?' They just stood there. 'Then who are you going to mind from now on?'

After a while, one of them said, 'You, Missy.'

'All right,' Granny said. 'Now listen to me. Go home. And if I ever hear of any of you straggling off like this again, I'll see to it. Now line up and come up here one at a time while we divide the food.'

It took a long time until the last one was gone; when we started again, we had almost enough mules for everybody to ride, but not quite, and Ringo drove now. He didn't ask; he just got in and took the reins, with Granny on the seat by him; it was just once that she told him not to go so fast. So I rode in the back then, on one of the chests, and that afternoon I was asleep; it was the wagon stopping that woke me. We had just come down a hill on to a flat, and then I saw them beyond a field, about a dozen of them, cavalry in blue coats. They hadn't seen us yet, trotting along, while Granny and Ringo watched them.

'They ain't hardly worth fooling with,' Ringo said. 'Still, they's horses.'

'We've already got a hundred and ten,' Granny said. 'That's all the paper calls for.'

'All right,' Ringo said. 'You wanter go on?' Granny didn't

answer, sitting there drawn back a little, with her hand at her breast again. 'Well, what you wanter do?' Ringo said. 'You got to 'cide quick, or they be gone.' He looked at her; she didn't move. Ringo leaned out of the wagon. 'Hey!' he hollered. They looked back quick and saw us and whirled about. 'Granny say come here!' Ringo hollered.

'You, Ringo,' Granny whispered.

'All right,' Ringo said. 'You want me to tell um to never mind?' She didn't answer; she was looking past Ringo at the two Yankees who were riding towards us across the field with that kind of drawnback look on her face and her hand holding the front of her dress. It was a lieutenant and a sergeant; the lieutenant didn't look much older than Ringo and me. He saw Granny and took off his hat. And then all of a sudden she took her hand away from her chest; it had the paper in it; she held it out to the lieutenant without saying a word. The lieutenant opened it, the sergeant looking over his shoulder. Then the sergeant looked at us.

'This says mules, not horses,' he said.

'Just the first hundred was mules,' Ringo said. 'The extra twelve is horses.'

'Damn it!' the lieutenant said. He sounded like a girl swearing. 'I told Captain Bowen not to mount us with captured stock!'

'You mean you're going to give them the horses?' the sergeant said.

'What else can I do?' the lieutenant said. He looked like he was fixing to cry. 'It's the general's own signature!'

So then we had enough stock for all of them to ride except about fifteen or twenty. We went on. The soldiers stood under a tree by the road, with their saddles and bridles on the ground beside them – all but the lieutenant. When we started again, he ran along by the wagon; he looked like he was going to cry, trotting along by the wagon with his hat in his hand, looking at Granny.

'You'll meet some troops somewhere,' he said. 'I know you will. Will you tell them where we are and to send us something – mounts or wagons – anything we can ride in? You won't forget?'

'They's some of yawl about twenty or thirty miles back that claim to have three extry mules,' Ringo said. 'But when we sees any more of um, we'll tell um about yawl.'

We went on. We came in sight of a town, but we went around it; Ringo didn't even want to stop and send the lieutenant's message in, but Granny made him stop and we sent the message in by one of the niggers.

'That's one more mouth to feed we got shed of,' Ringo said.

We went on. We went fast now, changing the mules every few miles; a woman told us we were in Mississippi again, and then, in the afternoon, we came over the hill, and there our chimneys were, standing up into the sunlight, and the cabin behind them and Louvinia bending over a washtub and the clothes on the line, flapping bright and peaceful.

'Stop the wagon,' Granny said.

We stopped – the wagon, the hundred and twenty-two mules and horses, and the niggers we never had had time to count.

Granny got out slow and turned to Ringo. 'Get out,' she said; then she looked at me. 'You too,' she said. 'Because you said nothing at all.' We got out of the wagon. She looked at us. 'We have lied,' she said.

'Hit was the paper that lied; hit wasn't us,' Ringo said.

'The paper said a hundred and ten. We have a hundred and twenty-two,' Granny said. 'Kneel down.'

'But they stole them 'fore we did,' Ringo said.

'But we lied,' Granny said. 'Kneel down.' She knelt first. Then we all three knelt by the road while she prayed. The washing blew soft and peaceful and bright on the clothesline. And then Louvinia saw us; she was already running across the pasture while Granny was praying.

Riposte in Tertio

I

When Ab Snopes left for Memphis with the nine mules, Ringo and Joby and I worked on a new fence. Then Ringo went off on his mule and there was just Joby and me. Once Granny came down and looked at the new section of rails; the pen would be almost two acres larger now. That was the second day after Ringo left. That night, while Granny and I were sitting before the fire, Ab Snopes came back. He said that he had got only four hundred and fifty dollars for the nine mules. That is, he took some money out of his pocket and gave it to Granny, and she counted it and said:

'That's only fifty dollars apiece.'

'All right,' Ab said. 'If you can do any better, you are welcome to take the next batch in yourself. I done already admitted I can't hold a candle to you when it comes to getting mules; maybe I can't even compete with you when it comes to selling them.' He chewed something – tobacco when he could get it, willow bark when he couldn't – all the time, and he never wore a collar, and nobody ever admitted they ever saw him in a uniform, though when Father was away, he would talk a lot now and then about when he was in Father's troop and about what he and Father used to do. But when I asked Father about it once, Father said, 'Who? Ab Snopes?' and then laughed. But it was Father that told Ab to kind of look out for Granny while he was away; only he told me and Ringo to look out for Ab, too, that Ab was all right in his way, but he was like a mule: while you had him in the traces, you better watch him. But Ab and Granny got along all right, though each time Ab took a batch of mules to Memphis and came back with the money, it would be like this: 'Yes, ma'am,' Ab said. 'It's easy to talk about hit, setting here without no risk. But I'm the one that has to dodge them durn critters nigh a hundred miles into Memphis, with Forrest and Smith fighting on every side of me and me never knowing when I wull run into a Confed'rit or Yankee patrol and have ever last one of them confiscated off of me right

84

down to the durn halters. And then I got to take them into the very heart of the Yankee Army in Memphis and try to sell them to a e-quipment officer that's liable at any minute to recognize them as the same mules he bought from me not two weeks ago. Yes. Hit's easy enough for them to talk that sets here getting rich and takes no risk.'

'I suppose you consider getting them back for you to sell taking no risk,' Granny said.

'The risk of running out of them printed letterheads, sho,' Ab said. 'If you ain't satisfied with making just five or six hundred dollars at a time, why don't you requisition for more mules at a time? Why don't you write out a letter and have General Smith turn over his commissary train to you, with about four wagonloads of new shoes in hit? Or, better than that, pick out the day when the pay officer is coming around and draw for the whole pay wagon; then we wouldn't even have to bother about finding somebody to buy hit.'

The money was in new bills. Granny folded them carefully and put them into the can, but she didn't put the can back inside her dress right away [and she never put it back under the loose board beneath her bed while Ab was about the place). She sat there looking at the fire, with the can in her hands and the string which suspended it looping down from around her neck. She didn't look any thinner or any older. She didn't look sick either. She just looked like somebody that has quit sleeping at night.

'We have more mules,' she said, 'if you would just sell them. There are more than a hundred of them that you refuse – '

'Refuse is right,' Ab said; he began to holler now: 'Yes, sir! I reckon I ain't got much sense, or I wouldn't be doing this a-tall. But I got better sense than to take them mules to a Yankee officer and tell him that them hip patches where you and that durn nigger burned out the U.S. brand are trace galls. By Godfrey, I – '

'That will do,' Granny said. 'Have you had some supper?'

'I – ' Ab said. Then he quit hollering. He chewed again. 'Yessum,' he said. 'I done et.'

'Then you had better go home and get some rest,' Granny said. 'There is a new relief regiment at Mottstown. Ringo went down two days ago to see about it. So we may need that new fence soon.'

Ab stopped chewing. 'Is, huh?' he said. 'Out of Memphis, likely. Likely got them nine mules in it we just got shet of.'

Granny looked at him. 'So you sold them further back than three days ago, then,' Granny said. Ab started to say something, but Granny didn't give him time. 'You go on home and rest up,' she said. 'Ringo will probably be back tomorrow, and then you'll have a chance to see if they are the same mules. I may even have a chance to find out what they say they paid you for them.'

Ab stood in the door and looked at Granny. 'You're a good un,' he said. 'Yessum. You got my respect. John Sartoris, himself, can't tech you. He hells all over the country day and night with a hundred armed men, and it's all he can do to keep them in crowbait to ride on. And you set here in this cabin, without nothing but a handful of durn printed letterheads, and you got to build a bigger pen to hold the stock you ain't got no market yet to sell. How many head of mules have you sold back to the Yankees?'

'A hundred and five,' Granny said.

'A hundred and five,' Ab said. 'For how much active cash money, in round numbers?' Only he didn't wait for her to answer; he told her himself: 'For six thou-sand and seven hun-dred and twen-ty-two dollars and six-ty five cents, lessen the dollar and thirty-five cents I spent for whisky that time the snake bit one of the mules.' It sounded round when he said it, like big sawn-oak wheels running in wet sand. 'You started out a year ago with two. You got forty-odd in the pen and twice that many out on receipt. And I reckon you have sold about fifty-odd more back to the Yankees a hundred and five times, for a grand total of six thousand, seven hundred and twenty-two dollars and sixty-five cents, and in a day or so you are aiming to requisition a few of them back again, I under-stand.'

He looked at me. 'Boy,' he said, 'when you grow up and start out for yourself, don't you waste your time learning to be a lawyer or nothing. You must save your money and buy you a handful of printed letterheads – it don't matter much what's on them, I reckon – and you hand them to your grandmaw here and just ask her to give you the job of counting the money when hit comes in.'

He looked at Granny again. 'When Kernel Sartoris left here, he told me to look out for you against General Grant and them. What I wonder is, if somebody hadn't better tell Abe Lincoln to look out for General Grant against Miz Rosa Millard. I bid you one and all good-night.'

He went out. Granny looked at the fire, the tin can in her hand. But it didn't have any six thousand dollars in it. It didn't have a thousand dollars in it. Ab Snopes knew that, only I don't suppose that it was possible for him to believe it. Then she got up; she looked at me, quiet. She didn't look sick; that wasn't it. 'I reckon it's bedtime,' she said. She went beyond the quilt; it came back and hung straight down from the rafter, and I heard the loose board when she put the can away under the floor, and then I heard the sound the bed made when she would hold to the post to kneel down. It would make another sound when she got up, but when it made that sound, I was already undressed and in my pallet. The quilts were cold, but when the sound came I had been there long enough for them to begin to get warm.

Ab Snopes came and helped me and Joby with the new fence the next day, so we finished it early in the afternoon and I went back to the cabin. I was almost there when I saw Ringo on the mule turning in at the gates. Granny had seen him, too, because when I went inside the quilt, she was kneeling in the corner, taking the window shade from under the loose floorboard. While she was unrolling the shade on the bed we heard Ringo getting off the mule, hollering at it while he hitched it to Louvinia's clothesline.

Then Granny stood up and looked at the quilt until Ringo pushed it aside and came in. And then they sounded like two people playing a guessing game in code.

'—th Illinois Infantry,' Ringo said. He came on towards the map on the bed. 'Col. G. W. Newberry. Eight days out of Memphis.'

Granny watched him while he came towards the bed. 'How many?' she said.

'Nineteen head,' Ringo said. 'Four with; fifteen without.' Granny just watched him; she didn't have to speak at all for the next one. 'Twelve,' Ringo said. 'Out of that Oxford batch.' Granny looked at the map; they both looked at it. 'July the twenty-second,' Granny said.

'Yessum,' Ringo said. Granny sat down on the saw chunk before the map. It was the only window shade Louvinia had; Ringo had drawn it (Father was right; he was smarter than me; he had even learned to draw, who had declined even to try to learn to print his name when Loosh was teaching me; who had learned to draw immediately by merely taking up the pen, who had no affinity for it and never denied he had not but who learned to draw simply because somebody had to) with Granny showing him where to draw in the towns. But it was Granny who had done the writing, in her neat spidery hand like she wrote in the cookbook with, written on the map by each town: *Colonel* or *Major* or *Captain So-and-So, Such-and-Such Regiment* or *Troop*. Then, under that: 12 or 9 or 21 *mules*. And around four of them, town and writing and all, in purple pokeberry juice instead of ink, a circle with a date in it, and in big neat letters *Complete*.

They looked at the map, Granny's head white and still where the light came through the window on it, and Ringo leaning over her. He had got taller during the summer; he was taller than me now, maybe from the exercise of riding around the country, listening out for fresh regiments with mules, and he had got to treating me like Granny did – like he and Granny were the same age instead of him and me.

'We just sold that twelve in July,' Granny said. 'That leaves only seven. And you say that four of them are branded.'

'That was back in July,' Ringo said. 'It's October now. They done forgot about hit. 'Sides, look here' – he put his finger on the map. 'We captived these here fourteen at Madison on the twelf of April, sont um to Memphis and sold um, and had all fourteen back and three more besides, here at Caledonia on the third of May.'

'But that was four counties apart,' Granny said. 'Oxford and Mottstown are only a few miles apart.'

'Phut,' Ringo said, 'these folks is too busy keeping us conquered to recognize no little ten or twelve head of stock. 'Sides, if they does recognize um in Memphis, that's Ab Snope's trouble, not ourn.'

'Mister Snopes,' Granny said.

'All right,' Ringo said. He looked at the map. 'Nineteen head, and not two days away. Jest forty-eight hours to have um in the pen.'

Granny looked at the map. 'I don't think we ought to risk it. We have been successful so far. Too successful perhaps.'

'Nineteen head,' Ringo said. 'Four to keep and fifteen to sell back to um. That will make a even two hundred and forty-eight head of Confed'rit mules we done recovered and collected interest on, let alone the money.'

'I don't know what to do,' Granny said. 'I want to think about it.'

'All right,' Ringo said. Granny sat still beside the map. Ringo didn't seem patient or impatient either; he just stood there, thin and taller than me against the light from the window, scratching himself. Then he began to dig with his right-hand little fingernail between his front teeth; he looked at his fingernail and spat something, and then he said, 'Must been five minutes now.' He turned his head a little towards me without moving. 'Get the pen and ink,' he said.

They kept the paper under the same floorboard with the map and the tin can. I don't know how or where Ringo got it. He just came back one night with about a hundred sheets of it, stamped with the official letterhead: UNITED STATES FORCES. DEPARTMENT OF TENNESSEE. He had got the pen and the ink at the same time, too; he took them from me, and now it was Ringo sitting on the saw chuck and Granny leaning over him. Granny still had the first letter – the order that Colonel Dick had given us in Alabama last year – she kept it in the can, too, and by now Ringo had learned to copy it so that I don't believe that Colonel Dick himself could have told the difference. All they had to do was to put in the right regiment and whatever number of mules Ringo had examined and approved, and sign the right general's name to it. At first Ringo had wanted to sign Grant's name every time, and when Granny said that would not do any more, Lincoln's. At last Granny

89

found out that Ringo objected to having the Yankees think that Father's folks would have any dealings with anybody under the General-in-Chief. But at last he realized that Granny was right, that they would have to be careful about what general's name was on the letter, as well as what mules they requisitioned. They were using General Smith now; he and Forrest were fighting every day up and down the road to Memphis, and Ringo always remembered to put in rope.

He wrote the date and the town, the headquarters; he wrote in Colonel Newberry's name and the first line. Then he stopped; he didn't lift the pen.

'What name you want this time?' he said.

'I'm worried about this,' Granny said. 'We ought not to risk it.'

'We was on "F" last time,' Ringo said. 'It's "H" now. Think of a name in "H".'

'Mrs Mary Harris,' Granny said.

'We done used Mary before,' Ringo said. 'How about Plurella Harris?'

'I'm worried about this time,' Granny said.

'Miz Plurella Harris,' Ringo said, writing. 'Now we done used up "P" too. 'Member that, now. I reckon when we run out of letters, maybe we can start in on numbers. We will have nine hundred and ninety-nine before we have to worry, then.' He finished the order and signed 'General Smith' to it; it looked exactly like the man who had signed the one Colonel Dick gave us was named General Smith, except for the number of mules. Then Granny turned and looked at me.

'Tell Mr Snopes to be ready at sunup,' she said.

We went in the wagon, with Ab Snopes and his two men following on two of the mules. We went just fast enough so that we would reach the bivouac at suppertime, because Granny and Ringo had found out that that was the best time – that the stock would all be handy, and the men would be too hungry or sleepy or something to think very quick in case they happened to think, and we would just have time to get the mules and get out of sight before dark came. Then, if they should decide to chase us, by the time they found us in the dark, there wouldn't be anything but the wagon with me and Granny in it to capture.

So we did; only this time it was a good thing we did. We left Ab Snopes and his men in the woods beyond the bivouac, and Granny and Ringo and I drove up to Colonel Newberry's tent at exactly the right time, and Granny passed the sentry and went into the tent, walking thin and straight, with the shawl over her shoulders and Mrs Compson's hat on her head and the parasol in one hand and hers and Ringo's General Smith order in the other, and Ringo and I sat in the wagon and looked at the cook fires about the grove and smelled the coffee and the meat. It was always the same. Granny would disappear into the tent or the house, and then, in about a minute, somebody would holler inside the tent or the house, and then the sentry at the door would holler, and then a sergeant, or even sometimes an officer, only it would be a lieutenant, would hurry into the tent or the house, and then Ringo and I would hear somebody cursing, and then they would all come out, Granny walking straight and stiff and not looking much bigger than Cousin Denny at Hawkhurst, and three or four mad Yankee officers behind her, and getting madder all the time. Then they would bring up the mules, tied together, Granny and Ringo could guess to the second now; it would be just enough light left to tell that they were mules, and Granny would get into the wagon and Ringo would hang his legs over the tail gate, holding the lead rope, and we would go on, not fast, so that when we came back to where Ab Snopes and his men waited in the woods you could not even tell that they were mules. Then Ringo would get on to the lead mule and they would turn off into the woods and Granny and I would go on home.

That's what we did this time; only this time it happened. We couldn't even see our own team when we heard them coming, the galloping hoofs. They came up fast and mad; Granny jerked up quick and straight, holding Mrs Compson's parasol.

'Damn that Ringo!' she said. 'I had my doubts about this time all the while.'

Then they were all around us, like the dark itself had fallen down on us, full of horses and mad men shouting 'Halt! Halt! If they try to escape, shoot the team!' with me and Granny sitting in the wagon and men jerking the team back and the team jerking and clashing in the traces, and some of them hollering 'Where are the mules? The mules are gone!' and the officer cursing and shouting 'Of course they are gone!' and cursing Granny and the darkness and the men and mules. Then somebody struck a light and we saw the officer sitting his horse beside the wagon while one of the soldiers lit one light-wood splinter from another.

'Where are the mules?' the officer shouted.

'What mules?' Granny said.

'Don't lie to me!' the officer shouted. 'The mules you just left camp with on that forged order! We have got you this time! We knew you'd turn up again. Orders went out to the whole department to watch for you a month ago! That damn Newberry had his copy in his pocket while you were talking to him.' He cursed Colonel Newberry now. 'They ought to let you go free and court-martial him! Where's the nigger boy and the mules, Mrs Plurella Harris?'

'I don't know what you are talking about,' Granny said. 'I have no mules except this team I am driving. And my name is Rosa Millard. I am on my way home beyond Jefferson.'

The officer began to laugh; he sat on the horse, laughing. 'So that's your real name, hey? Well, well, well. So you have begun to tell the truth at last. Come now, tell me where those mules are, and tell me where the others you have stolen from us are hid.'

Then Ringo hollered. He and Ab Snopes and the mules had turned off into the woods on the right side of the road, but when he hollered now he was on the left side. 'Heyo the road!' he hollered. 'One busted loose! Head um off the road!'

And that was all of that. The soldier dropped the light-wood splinter and the officer whirled his horse, already spurring him, hollering, 'Two men stay here.' Maybe they all thought he meant two others, because there was just a big noise of bushes and trees like a cyclone was going through them, and then Granny and I were sitting in the wagon like before we had even heard the hoofs.

'Come on,' Granny said. She was already getting out of the wagon.

'Are we going to leave the team and wagon?' I said.

'Yes,' Granny said. 'I misdoubted this all the time.'

We could not see at all in the woods; we felt our way, and me helping Granny along and her arm didn't feel any bigger than a pencil almost, but it wasn't trembling. 'This is far enough,' she said. I found a log and we sat down. Beyond the road we could hear them, thrashing around, shouting and cursing. It sounded far away now. 'And the team too,' Granny said.

'But we have nineteen new ones,' I said. 'That makes two hundred and forty-eight.' It seemed like a long time, sitting there on the log in the dark. After a while they came back, we could hear the officer cursing and the horses crashing and thumping back into the road. And then he found the wagon was empty and he cursed sure enough – Granny and me, and the two men he had told to stay there. He was still cursing while they turned the wagon around. Then they went away. After a while we couldn't hear them. Granny got up and we felt our way back to the road, and we went on, too, towards home. After a while I persuaded her to stop and rest, and while we were sitting beside the road we heard the buggy coming. We stood up, and Ringo saw us and stopped the buggy.

'Did I holler loud enough?' he said.

'Yes,' Granny said. Then she said, 'Well?'

'All right,' Ringo said. 'I told Ab Snopes to hide out with them in Hickahala bottom until tomorrow night. All 'cep' these two.'

'Mister Snopes,' Granny said.

'All right,' Ringo said. 'Get in and le's go home.'

Granny didn't move; I knew why, even before she spoke. 'Where did you get this buggy?'

'I borrowed hit,' Ringo said. ''Twarn't no Yankees handy, so I never needed no paper.'

We got in. The buggy went on. It seemed to me like it had already been all night, but it wasn't midnight yet – I could tell by the stars – we would be home by midnight almost. We went on. 'I reckon you went and told um who we is now,' Ringo said.

'Yes,' Granny said.

'Well, I reckon that completes that,' Ringo said. 'Anyway, we handled two hundred and forty-eight head while the business lasted.'

'Two hundred and forty-six,' Granny said. 'We have lost the team.'

2

It was after midnight when we reached home; it was already Sunday and when we reached the church that morning there was the biggest crowd waiting there had ever been, though Ab Snopes would not get back with the new mules until to-morrow. So I believed that somehow they had heard about last night and they knew too, like Ringo, that this was the end and that now the books would have to be balanced and closed. We were late, because Granny made Ringo get up at sunup and take the buggy back where he had got it. So when we reached the church they were already inside, waiting. Brother Fortin-bride met us at the door, and they all turned in the pews and watched Granny – the old men and the women and the children and the maybe a dozen niggers that didn't have any white people now – they looked at her exactly like Father's foxhounds would look at him when he would go into the dog run, while we went up the aisle to our pew. Ringo had the book; he went up to the gallery; I looked back and saw him leaning his arms on the book on the balustrade.

We sat down in our pew, like before there was a war, only for Father – Granny still and straight in her Sunday calico dress and the shawl and the hat Mrs Compson had loaned her a year ago; straight and quiet, with her hands holding her prayer book in her lap like always, though there hadn't been an Episcopal service in the church in almost three years now. Brother Fortin-bride was a Methodist, and I don't know what the people were. Last summer when we got back with the first batch of mules from Alabama, Granny sent for them, sent out word back into the hills where they lived in dirt-floored cabins, on the little poor farms without slaves. It took three or four times to get them to come in, but at last they all came – men and women and children and the dozen niggers that had got free by accident and didn't know what to do about it. I reckon this was the first church with a slave gallery some of them had ever seen, with Ringo and the other twelve sitting up there in the high shadows where there was room enough for two hundred; and I could remember back when Father would be in the pew with us and the grove outside would be full of carriages from the other plantations, and Doctor Worsham in his stole beneath the altar, and for each white person in the auditorium there would be ten niggers in the gallery. And I reckon that on that first Sunday when Granny knelt down in public, it was the first time they had ever seen anyone kneel in a church.

Brother Fortinbride wasn't a minister either. He was a private in Father's regiment, and he got hurt bad in the first battle the regiment was in; they thought that he was dead, but he said that Jesus came to him and told him to rise up and live, and Father sent him back home to die, only he didn't die. But they said that he didn't have any stomach left at all, and everybody thought that the food we had to eat in 1862 and 63 would finish killing him, even if he had eaten it with women to cook it instead of gathering weeds from ditch banks and cooking them himself. But it didn't kill him, and so maybe it was Jesus, after all, like he said. And so, when we came back with the first batch of mules and the silver and the food, and Granny sent word out for all that needed, it was like Brother Fortinbride sprang right up out of the ground with the names and histories of all the hill folks at his tongue's end, like maybe what he claimed was true – that the Lord had both him and Granny in mind when He created the other. So he would stand there where Doctor Worsham used to stand, and talk quiet for a little while about God, with his hair showing where he cut it himself and the bones looking like they were coming right out through his face, in a frock coat that had turned green a long time ago and with patches on it that he had sewed on himself – one of them was green horsehide and the other was a piece of tent canvas with the U.S.A. stencil still showing a little on it. He never talked long; there wasn't much anybody could say about Confederate armies now. I reckon there is a time when even preachers quit believing that God is going to change His plan and give victory where there is nothing left to hang victory on. He just said how victory without God is mockery and delusion, but that defeat with God is not defeat. Then he quit talking, and he stood there with the old men and the women and children and the eleven or twelve niggers lost in freedom, in clothes made out of cotton bagging and flour-sacks, still watching Granny – only now it was not like the hounds used to look at Father, but like they would watch the food in Loosh's hands when he would go in to feed them – and then he said:

'Brethren and sisters, Sister Millard wishes to bear public witness.'

Granny stood up. She would not go to the altar; she just stood there in our pew with her face straight ahead, in the shawl and Mrs Compson's hat and the dress that Louvinia washed and ironed every Saturday, holding the prayer book. It used to have her name on it in gold letters, but now the only way you could read them was to run your finger over them; she said quiet, too – quiet as Brother Fortinbride – 'I have sinned. I want you all to pray for me.'

She knelt down in the pew; she looked littler than Cousin Denny; it was only Mrs Compson's hat above the pew back they had to look at now. I don't know if she prayed herself or not. And Brother Fortinbride didn't pray either – not aloud anyway. Ringo and I were just past fifteen then, but I could imagine what Doctor Worsham would have thought up to say – about all soldiers did not carry arms, and about they also serve, and how one child saved from hunger and cold is better in heaven's sight than a thousand slain enemies. But Brother Fortinbride didn't say it. I reckon he thought of that; he always had plenty of words when he wanted to. It was like he said to himself, 'Words are fine in peacetime, when everybody is comfortable and easy. But now I think that we can be excused.' He just stood there where Doctor Worsham used to stand and where the bishop would stand, too, with his ring looking big as a pistol target. Then Granny rose up; I didn't have time to help her; she stood up, and then the long sound went through the church, a sound kind of like a sigh that Ringo said was the sound of the cotton bagging and the floursacking when they breathed again, and Granny turned and looked back towards the gallery; only Ringo was already moving.

'Bring the book,' she said.

It was a big blank account book; it weighed almost fifteen pounds. They opened it on the reading desk, Granny and

Ringo side by side, while Granny drew the tin can out of her dress and spread the money on the book. But nobody moved until she began to call out the names. Then they came up one at a time, while Ringo read the names off the book, and the date, and the amount they had received before. Each time Granny would make them tell what they intended to do with the money, and now she would make them tell her how they had spent it, and she would look at the book to see whether they had lied or not. And the ones that she had loaned the brand-blotted mules that Ab Snopes was afraid to try to sell would have to tell her how the mule was getting along and how much work it had done, and now and then she would take the mule away from one man or woman and give it to another, tearing up the old receipt and making the man or the woman sign the new one, telling them on what day to go and get the mule.

So it was afternoon when Ringo closed the book and got the new receipts together, and Granny stopped putting the rest of the money back into the can and she and Brother Fortinbride did what they did each time. 'I'm making out fine with the mule,' he said. 'I don't need any money.'

'Fiddlesticks,' Granny said. 'You'll never grow enough food out of the ground to feed a bird the longest day you live. You take this money.'

'No,' Brother Fortinbride said. 'I'm making out fine.'

We walked back home, Ringo carrying the book. 'You done receipted out four mules you ain't hardly laid eyes on yet,' he said. 'What you gonter do about that?'

'They will be here tomorrow morning, I reckon,' Granny said. They were; Ab Snopes came in while we were eating breakfast; he leaned in the door with his eyes a little red from lack of sleep and looked at Granny.

'Yes, ma'am,' he said, 'I don't never want to be rich; I just want to be lucky. Do you know what you done?' Only nobody asked him what, so he told us anyway: 'Hit was taking place all day yestiddy; I reckon by now there ain't a Yankee regiment left in Mississippi. You might say that this here war has turned around at last and went back North. Yes, sir. The regiment you requisitioned on Sattidy never even stayed long enough to warm the ground. You managed to requisition the last batch of

Yankee livestock at the last possible moment hit could have been done by living man. You made just one mistake: You drawed them last nineteen mules just too late to have anybody to sell them back to.'

3

It was a bright warm day; we saw the guns and the bits shining a long way down the road. But this time Ringo didn't even move. He just quit drawing and looked up from the paper and said, 'So Ab Snopes was lying. Gre't God, ain't we gonter never get shet of them?'

It was just a lieutenant; by this time Ringo and I could tell the different officers' ranks better than we could tell Confederate ranks, because one day we counted up and the only Confederate officers we had ever seen were Father and the captain that talked to us with Uncle Buck McCaslin that day in Jefferson before Grant burned it. And this was to be the last time we would see any uniforms at all except as the walking symbols of defeated men's pride and indomitable unregret, but we didn't know that now.

So it was just a lieutenant. He looked about forty, and kind of mad and gleeful, both at the same time. Ringo didn't recognize him because he had not been in the wagon with us, but I did – from the way he sat the horse, or maybe from the way he looked mad and happy both, like he had been mad for several days, thinking about how much he was going to enjoy being mad when the right time came. And he recognized me, too; he looked at me once and said 'Hah!' with his teeth showing, and pushed his horse up and looked at Ringo's picture. There were maybe a dozen cavalry behind him; we never noticed especially. 'Hah!' he said again, then he said, 'What's that?'

'A house,' Ringo said. Ringo had never even looked at him good yet; he had seen even more of them than I had. 'Look at it.'

The lieutenant looked at me and said 'Hah!' again behind his teeth; every now and then while he was talking to Ringo he would do that. He looked at Ringo's picture. Then he looked up the grove to where the chimneys rose out of the pile of rubble and ashes. Grass and weeds had come up out of the ashes now, and unless you knew better, all you saw was the four chimneys. Some of the goldenrod was still in bloom. 'Oh,' the officer said. 'I see. You're drawing it like it used to be.'

'Co-rect,' Ringo said. 'What I wanter draw hit like hit is now? I can walk down here ten times a day and look at hit like hit is now. I can even ride in that gate on a horse and do that.'

The lieutenant didn't say 'Hah!' this time. He didn't do any-thing yet; I reckon he was still enjoying waiting a little longer to get good and mad. He just kind of grunted. 'When you get done here, you can move into town and keep busy all winter, can't you?' he said. Then he sat back in the saddle. He didn't say 'Hah!' now either; it was his eyes that said it, looking at me. They were a kind of thin milk colour, like the chine knuckle-bone in a ham. 'All right,' he said. 'Who lives up there now? What's her name today, hey?'

Ringo was watching him now, though I don't think he sus-pected yet who he was. 'Don't nobody,' he said. 'The roof leaks.' One of the men made a kind of sound; maybe it was laughing. The lieutenant started to whirl around, and then he started not to; then he sat there glaring down at Ringo with his mouth beginning to open. 'Oh,' Ringo said, 'you mean way back yonder in the quarters. I thought you was still worrying about them chimneys.'

This time the soldier did laugh, and this time the lieutenant did whirl around, cursing at the soldier; I would have known him now even if I hadn't before. He cursed at them all now, sitting there with his face swelling up. 'Blank-blank-blank!' he shouted. 'Get to hell on out of here! He said that pen is down there in the creek bottom beyond the pasture. If you meet man, woman or child and they so much as smile at you, shoot them! Get!' The soldiers went on, galloping up the drive; we watched them scatter out across the pasture. The lieutenant looked at me and Ringo; he said 'Hah!' again, glaring at us. 'You boys come with me. Jump!'

He didn't wait for us; he galloped, too, up the drive. We ran; Ringo looked at me. '"He" said the pen was in the creek bottom,' Ringo said. 'Who you reckon "he" is?'

'I don't know,' I said.

'Well, I reckon I know,' Ringo said. But we didn't talk any more. We ran on up the drive. The lieutenant had reached the cabin now, and Granny came out the door. I reckon she had seen him, too, because she already had her sunbonnet on. They looked at us once, then Granny went on, too, walking straight, not fast, down the path towards the lot, with the lieutenant behind her on the horse. We could see his shoulders and his head and now and then his hand and arm, but we couldn't hear what he was saying. 'I reckon this does complete hit,' Ringo said.

But we could hear him before we reached the new fence. Then we could see them standing at the fence that Joby and I had just finished – Granny straight and still, with her sunbonnet on and the shawl drawn tight over her shoulders where she had her arms folded in it so that she looked littler than anybody I could remember, like during the four years she hadn't got any older or weaker, but just littler and littler and straighter and straighter and more and more indomitable; and the lieutenant beside her with one hand on his hip and waving a whole handful of letters at Granny's face with the other.

'Look like he got all we ever wrote there,' Ringo said. The soldiers' horses were all tied along the fence; they were inside the pen now, and they and Joby and Ab Snopes had the forty-odd old mules and the nineteen new ones hemmed into the corner. The mules were still trying to break out, only it didn't look like that. It looked like every one of them was trying to keep the big burned smear where Granny and Ringo had blotted the U.S. brand turned so that the lieutenant would have to look at it.

'And I guess you will call those scars left-handed trace galls!' the lieutenant said. 'You have been using cast-off band-saw bands for traces, hey? I'd rather engage Forrest's whole brigade every morning for six months than spend that same length of time trying to protect United States property from defenceless Southern women and niggers and children. Defenceless!' he shouted. 'Defenceless! God help the North if Davis and Lee had ever thought of the idea of forming a brigade of grandmothers and nigger orphans, and invading us with it!' he hollered, shaking the letters at Granny.

In the pen the mules huddled and surged, with Ab Snopes waving his arms at them now and then. Then the lieutenant quit shouting; he even quit shaking the letters at Granny.

'Listen,' he said. 'We are on evacuation orders now. Likely I am the last Federal soldier you will have to look at. And I'm not going to harm you – orders to that effect too. All I'm going to do is take back this stolen property. And now I want you to tell me, as enemy to enemy, or even man to man, if you like. I know from these forged orders how many head of stock you have taken from us, and I know from the records how many times you have sold a few of them back to us; I even know what we paid you. But how many of them did you actually sell back to us more than one time?'

'I don't know,' Granny said.

'You don't know,' the lieutenant said. He didn't start to shout now, he just stood there, breathing slow and hard, look-ing at Granny; he talked now with a kind of furious patience, as if she were an idiot or an Indian: 'Listen. I know you don't have to tell me, and you know I can't make you. I ask it only out of pure respect. Respect? Envy. Won't you tell me?'

'I don't know,' Granny said.

'You don't know,' the lieutenant said. 'You mean, you – ' He talked quiet now. 'I see. You really don't know. You were too busy running the reaper to count the – ' We didn't move. Granny wasn't even looking at him; it was Ringo and me that watched him fold the letters that Granny and Ringo had written and put them carefully into his pocket. He still talked quiet, like he was tired. 'All right, boys. Rope them together and haze them out of there.'

'The gate is a quarter of a mile from here,' a soldier said.

'Throw down some fence,' the lieutenant said. They began to throw down the fence that Joby and I had worked two months on. The lieutenant took a pad from his pocket, and he went to the fence and laid the pad on the rail and took out a pencil. Then he looked back at Granny; he still talked quiet: 'I believe you said the name now is Rosa Millard?'

'Yes,' Granny said.

The lieutenant wrote on the pad and tore the sheet out and came back to Granny. He still talked quiet, like when somebody is sick in a room. 'We are under orders to pay for all property damaged in the process of evacuation,' he said. 'This is a voucher on the quartermaster at Memphis for ten dollars. For the fence.' He didn't give the paper to her at once; he just stood there, looking at her. 'Confound it, I don't mean promise. If I just knew what you believed in, held – ' He cursed again, not loud and not at anybody or anything. 'Listen. I don't say promise; I never mentioned the word. But I have a family; I am a poor man; I have no grandmother. And if in about four months the auditor should find a warrant in the records for a thousand dollars to Mrs Rosa Millard, I would have to make it good. Do you see?'

'Yes,' Granny said. 'You need not worry.'

Then they were gone. Granny and Ringo and Joby and I stood there and watched them drive the mules up across the pasture and out of sight. We had forgot about Ab Snopes until he said, 'Well, hit looks like that's all they are to hit. But you still got that ere hundred-odd that are out on receipt, provided them hill folks don't take a example from them Yankees. I reckon you can still be grateful for that much anyway. So I'll bid you, one and all, good day and get on home and rest a spell. If I can help you again, just send for me.' He went on too.

After a while Granny said:

'Joby, put those rails back up.' I reckon Ringo and I were both waiting for her to tell us to help Joby, but she didn't. She just said 'Come,' and turned and went on, not towards the cabin but across the pasture towards the road. We didn't know where we were going until we reached the church. She went straight up the aisle to the chancel and stood there until we came up. 'Kneel down,' she said.

We knelt in the empty church. She was small between us, little; she talked quiet, not loud, not fast and not slow; her voice sounded quiet and still, but strong and clear: 'I have sinned. I have stolen, and I have borne false witness against my neighbour, though that neighbour was an enemy of my country. And more than that, I have caused these children to sin. I hereby take their sins upon my conscience.' It was one of those bright soft days. It was cool in the church; the floor was cold to my knees. There was a hickory branch just outside the window turning yellow; when the sun touched it, the leaves looked like gold. 'But I did not sin for gain or for greed,' Granny said. 'I did not sin for revenge. I defy You or anyone to say I did. I sinned first for justice. And after that first time, I sinned for more than justice; I sinned for the sake of food and clothes for Your own creatures who could not help themselves – for children who had given their fathers, for wives who had given their husbands, for old people who had given their sons to a holy cause, even though You have seen fit to make it a lost cause. What I gained, I shared with them. It is true that I kept some of it back, but I am the best judge of that because I, too, have dependants who may be orphans, too, at this moment, for all I know. And if this be sin in Your sight, I take this on my conscience too. Amen.'

She rose up. She got up easy, like she had no weight to herself. It was warm outside; it was the finest October that I could remember. Or maybe it was because you are not conscious of weather until you are fifteen. We walked slow back home, though Granny said she wasn't tired. 'I just wish I knew how they found out about that pen,' she said.

'Don't you know?' Ringo said. Granny looked at him. 'Ab Snopes told them.'

This time she didn't even say, 'Mister Snopes.' She just stopped dead still and looked at Ringo. 'Ab Snopes?'

'Do you reckon he was going to be satisfied until he had sold them last nineteen mules to somebody?' Ringo said.

'Ab Snopes,' Granny said. 'Well.' Then she walked on; we walked on. 'Ab Snopes,' she said. 'I reckon he beat me, after all. But it can't be helped now. And anyway, we did pretty well, taken by and large.'

'We done damn well,' Ringo said. He caught himself, but it was already too late. Granny didn't even stop.

'Go on home and get the soap,' she said.

He went on. We could watch him cross the pasture and go into the cabin, and then come out and go down the hill towards the spring. We were close now; when I left Granny and went down to the spring, he was just rinsing his mouth, the can of soap in one hand and the gourd dipper in the other. He spit and rinsed his mouth and spit again; there was a long smear of suds up his cheek; a light froth of coloured bubbles flicking away while I watched them, without any sound at all. 'I still says we done damn well,' he said.

4

We tried to keep her from doing it – we both tried. Ringo had told her about Ab Snopes, and after that we both knew it. It was like all three of us should have known it all the time. Only I don't believe now that he meant to happen what did happen. But I believe that if he had known what was going to happen, he would still have egged her on to do it. And Ringo and I tried – we tried – but Granny just sat there before the fire – it was cold in the cabin now – with her arms folded in the shawl and with that look on her face when she had quit either arguing or listening to you at all, saying just this one time more and that even a rogue will be honest for enough pay. It was Christmas; we had just heard from Aunt Louisa at Hawkhurst and found out where Drusilla was; she had been missing from home for almost a year now, and at last Aunt Louisa found out that she was with Father away in Carolina, like she had told me, riding with the troop like she was a man.

Ringo and I had just got back from Jefferson with the letter, and Ab Snopes was in the cabin, telling Granny about it, and Granny listening and believing him because she still believed that what side of a war a man fought on made him what he is. And she knew better with her own ears; she must have known; everybody knew about them and were either mad if they were men or terrified if they were women. There was one Negro in the county that everybody knew that they had murdered and burned him up in his cabin. They called themselves Grumby's Independents – about fifty or sixty of them that wore no uniform and came from nobody knew where as soon as the last Yankee regiment was out of the country, raiding smokehouses and stables, and houses where they were sure there were no men, tearing up beds and floors and walls, frightening white women and torturing Negroes to find where money or silver was hidden.

They were caught once, and the one that said he was Grumby

produced a tattered raiding commission actually signed by General Forrest; though you couldn't tell if the original name was Grumby or not. But it got them off, because it was just some old men that captured them; and now women who had lived alone for three years surrounded by invading armies were afraid to stay in the houses at night, and the Negroes who had lost their white people lived hidden in caves back in the hills like animals.

That's who Ab Snopes was talking about, with his hat on the floor and his hands flapping and his hair bent up across the back of his head where he had slept on it. The band had a thorough-bred stallion and three mares – how Ab Snopes knew it he didn't say – that they had stolen; and how he knew they were stolen, he didn't say. But all Granny had to do was to write out one of the orders and sign Forrest's name to it; he, Ab, would guarantee to get two thousand dollars for the horses. He swore to that, and Granny, sitting there with her arms rolled into the shawl and that expression on her face, and Ab Snopes' shadow leaping and jerking up the wall while he waved his arms and talked about that was all she had to do; to look at what she had made out of the Yankees, enemies, and that these were Southern men and, therefore, there would not even be any risk to this, because Southern men would not harm a woman, even if the letter failed to work.

Oh, he did it well. I can see now that Ringo and I had no chance against him – about how the business with the Yankees had stopped without warning, before she had made what she had counted on, and how she had given most of that away under the belief that she would be able to replace that and more, but as it was now, she had made independent and secure almost everyone in the county save herself and her own blood; that soon Father would return home to his ruined plantation and most of his slaves vanished; and how it would be if, when he came home and looked about at his desolate future, she could take fifteen hundred dollars in cash out of her pocket and say, 'Here. Start over with this' – fifteen hundred dollars more than she had hoped to have. He would take one of the mares for his commission and he would guarantee her fifteen hundred dollars for the other three.

Oh, we had no chance against him. We begged her to let us ask advice from Uncle Buck McCaslin, anyone, any man. But she just sat there with that expression on her face, saying that the horses did not belong to him, that they had been stolen, and that all she had to do was to frighten them with the order, and even Ringo and I knowing at fifteen that Grumby, or whoever he was, was a coward and that you might frighten a brave man, but that nobody dared frighten a coward; and Granny, sitting there without moving at all and saying, 'But the horses do not belong to them because they are stolen property,' and we said, 'Then no more will they belong to us,' and Granny said, 'But they do not belong to them.'

But we didn't quit trying; all that day – Ab Snopes had located them; it was an abandoned cotton compress on Talla-hatchie River, sixty miles away – while we rode in the rain in the wagon Ab Snopes got for us to use, we tried. But Granny just sat there on the seat between us, with the order signed by Ringo for General Forrest in the tin can under her dress and her feet on some hot bricks in a crokersack that we would stop every ten miles and build a fire in the rain and heat again, until we came to the crossroads, where Ab Snopes told us to leave the wagon and walk. And then she would not let me and Ringo go with her. 'You and Ringo look like men,' she said. 'They won't hurt a woman.' It had rained all day; it had fallen grey and steady and slow and cold on us all day long, and now it was like twilight had thickened it without being able to make it any greyer or colder. The crossroad was not a road any more; it was no more than a faint gash turning off at right angles into the bottom, so that it looked like a cave. We could see the hoof marks in it.

'Then you shan't go,' I said. 'I'm stronger than you are; I'll hold you.' I held her; her arm felt little and light and dry as a stick. But it wasn't that; her size and appearance had no more to do with it than it had in her dealings with the Yankees; she just turned and looked at me, and then I began to cry. I would be sixteen years old before another year was out, yet I sat there in the wagon, crying. I didn't even know when she freed her arm. And then she was out of the wagon, standing there looking at me in the grey rain and the grey darkening light.

'It's for all of us,' she said. 'For John and you and Ringo and Joby and Louvinia. So we will have something when John comes back home. You never cried when you knew he was going into a battle, did you? And now I am taking no risk; I am a woman. Even Yankees do not harm old women. You and Ringo stay here until I call you.'

We tried. I keep on saying that because I know now that I didn't. I could have held her, turned the wagon, driven away, holding her in it. I was fifteen, and for most of my life her face had been the first thing I saw in the morning and the last thing I saw at night, but I could have stopped her, and I didn't. I sat there in the wagon in the cold rain and let her walk on into the wet twilight and never come out of it again. How many of them there were in the cold compress, I don't know, and when and why they took fright and left, I don't know.

We just sat there in the wagon in that cold dissolving December twilight until at last I couldn't bear it any longer. Then Ringo and I were both running, trying to run, in the ankle-deep mud of that old road pocked with the prints of ingoing hoofs, but of no wheel, knowing that we had waited too long either to help her or to share in her defeat. Because there was no sound nor sign of life at all; just the huge rotting building with the grey afternoon dying wetly upon it, and then at the end of the hall a faint crack of light beneath a door.

I don't remember touching the door at all, because the room was a floor raised about two feet from the earth, so that I ran into the step and fell forward into and then through the door, on to my hands and knees in the room, looking at Granny. There was a tallow dip burning on a wooden box, but it was the powder I smelled, stronger even than the tallow. I couldn't seem to breathe for the smell of the powder, looking at Granny. She had looked little alive, but now she looked like she had collapsed, like she had been made out of a lot of little thin dry light sticks notched together and braced with cord, and now the cord had broken and all the little sticks had collapsed in a quiet heap on the floor, and somebody had spread a clean and faded calico dress over them.

Vendée

I

They all came in again when we buried Granny, Brother
Fortinbride and all of them – the old men and the women and
the children, and the niggers – the twelve who used to come in
when word would spread that Ab Snopes was back from
Memphis, and the hundred more who had returned to the
county since, who had followed the Yankees away and then
returned, to find their families and owners gone, to scatter into
the hills and live in caves and hollow trees like animals I suppose, not only with no one to depend on but with no one
depending on them, caring whether they returned or not or
lived or died or not: and that I suppose is the sum, the sharp
serpent's fang, of bereavement and loss – all coming in from the
hills in the rain. Only there were no Yankees in Jefferson now
so they didn't have to walk in; I could look across the grave
and beyond the other headstones and monuments and see the
dripping cedar grove full of mules with long black smears on
their hips where Granny and Ringo had burned out the U.S.
brand.

Most of the Jefferson people were there too, and there was
another preacher – a big preacher refugeeing from Memphis or
somewhere – and I found out how Mrs Compson and some of
them had arranged for him to preach the funeral. But Brother
Fortinbride didn't let him. He didn't tell him not to; he just
didn't say anything to him at all, he just acted like a grown person coming in where the children are getting ready to play a
game and telling the children that the game is all right but that
the grown folks need the room and the furniture for a while. He
came walking fast up from the grove where he had hitched his
mule with the others, with his gaunted face and his frock coat
with the horsehide and the Yankee-tent patches, into where the
town people were standing around under umbrellas with
Granny in the middle and the big refugeeing preacher with his
book already open and one of the Compson niggers holding an
umbrella over him and the rain splashing slow and cold and

grey on the umbrella and splashing slow on the yellow boards
where Granny was and into the dark red dirt beside the red
grave without splashing at all. Brother Fortinbride just walked
in and looked at the umbrellas and then at the hill people in
cotton bagging and split floursack clothes that didn't have
umbrellas, and went to Granny and said, 'Come, you men.'

The town men would have moved. Some of them did. Uncle
Buck McCaslin was the first man of them all, town and hill, to
come forward. By Christmas his rheumatism would be so bad
that he couldn't hardly lift his hand, but he was there now, with
his peeled hickory stick, shoving up through the hill men
with crokersacks tied over their heads and the town men with
umbrellas getting out of his way; then Ringo and I stood there
and watched Granny going down into the earth with the quiet
rain splashing on the yellow boards until they quit looking like
boards and began to look like water with thin sunlight reflected
in it, sinking away into the ground. Then the wet red dirt
began to flow into the grave, with the shovels darting and flicking slow and steady and the hill men waiting to take turns with
the shovels because Uncle Buck would not let anyone spell him
with his.

It didn't take long, and I reckon the refugeeing preacher
would have tried again even then, but Brother Fortinbride
didn't give him a chance. Brother Fortinbride didn't even put
down his shovel; he stood there leaning on it like he was in the
field, and he sounded just like he used to in the church when
Ab Snopes would be home from Memphis again – strong and
quiet and not loud:

'I don't reckon that Rosa Millard or anybody that ever knew
her has to be told where she has gone. And I don't reckon that
anybody that ever knew her would want to insult her by telling
her to rest anywhere in peace. And I reckon that God has
already seen to it that there are men, women and children, black,
white, yellow or red waiting for her to tend and worry over.
And so you folks go home. Some of you ain't come far, and you
came that distance in carriages with tops. But most of you
didn't, and it's by the grace of Rosa Millard that you didn't
come on foot. I'm talking to you. You have wood to cut and
split, at least. And what do you reckon Rosa Millard would say

about you all standing around here, keeping old folks and children out here in the rain?'

Mrs Compson asked me and Ringo to come home and live with her until Father came back, and some others did – I don't remember who – and then, when I thought they had all gone, I looked around, and there was Uncle Buck. He came up to us with one elbow jammed into his side and his beard drawn over to one side like it was another arm, and his eyes red and mad like he hadn't slept much, and holding his stick like he was fixing to hit somebody with it and he didn't much care who.

'What you boys going to do now?' he said.

The earth was loose and soft now, dark and red with rain, so that the rain didn't splash on Granny at all; it just dissolved slow and grey into the dark-red mound, so that after a while the mound began to dissolve, too, without changing shape, like the soft yellow colour of the boards had dissolved and stained up through the earth, and mound and boards and rain were all melting into one vague quiet reddish grey.

'I want to borrow a pistol,' I said.

He began to holler then, but quiet. Because he was older than us; it was like it had been at the old compress that night with Granny. 'Need me or not,' he hollered, 'by Godfrey, I'm going! You can't stop me! You mean to tell me you don't want me to go with you?'

'I don't care,' I said. 'I just want a pistol. Or a gun. Ours got burned up with the house.'

'All right!' he hollered. 'Me and the pistol, or you and this nigger horse thief and a fence rail. You ain't even got a poker at home, have you?'

'We got the bar'l of the musket yet,' Ringo said. 'I reckon that's all we'll need for Ab Snopes.'

'Ab Snopes?' Uncle Buck hollered. 'Do you think it's Ab Snopes this boy is thinking about? ... Hey?' he hollered, hollering at me now. 'Hey, boy?' It was changing all the time, with the slow grey rain lancing slow and grey and cold into the red earth, yet it did not change. It would be some time yet; it would be days and weeks and then months before it would be smooth and quiet and level with the other earth. Now Uncle

Buck was talking at Ringo and not hollering now. 'Catch my mule,' he said. 'I got the pistol in my britches.'

Ab Snopes lived back in the hills too. Uncle Buck knew where; it was midafternoon by then and we were riding up a long red hill between pines when Uncle Buck stopped. He and Ringo had crokersacks tied over their heads. Uncle Buck's hand-worn stick stuck out from under his sack with the rain shining on it like a long wax candle.

'Wait,' he said. 'I got a idea.' We turned from the road and came to a creek bottom; there was a faint path. It was dark under the trees and the rain didn't fall on us now; it was like the bare trees themselves were dissolving slow and steady and cold into the end of the December day. We rode in single file, in our wet clothes and in the wet ammonia steam of the mules.

The pen was just like the one he and Ringo and Joby and I had built at home, only smaller and better hidden; I reckon he had got the idea from ours. We stopped at the wet rails; they were still new enough for the split sides to be still yellow with sap, and on the far side of the pen there was something that looked like a yellow cloud in the twilight, until it moved. And then we saw that it was a claybank stallion and three mares.

'I thought so,' Uncle Buck said.

Because I was mixed up. Maybe it was because Ringo and I were tired and we hadn't slept much lately. Because the days were mixed up with the nights, all the while we had been riding I would keep on thinking how Ringo and I would catch it from Granny when we got back home, for going off in the rain without telling her. Because for a minute I sat there and looked at the horses and I believed that Ab Snopes was Grumby. But Uncle Buck begun to holler again.

'Him, Grumby?' he hollered. 'Ab Snopes? Ab Snopes? By Godfrey, if he was Grumby, if it was Ab Snopes that shot your grandmaw, I'd be ashamed to have it known. I'd be ashamed to be caught catching him. No, sir. He ain't Grumby; he's better than that.' He sat sideways on his mule with the sack over his head and his beard jerking and wagging out of it while he talked. 'He's the one that's going to show us where Grumby is. They just hid them horses here because they thought this would be the last place you boys would think to look for them.

And now Ab Snopes has went off with Grumby to get some more, since your grandmaw has gone out of business, as far as he is concerned. And thank Godfrey for that. It won't be a house or a cabin they will ever pass as long as Ab Snopes is with them, that he won't leave an indelible signature, even if it ain't nothing to capture but a chicken or a kitchen clock. By Godfrey, the one thing we don't want is to catch Ab Snopes.'

And we didn't catch him that night. We went back to the road and went on, and then we came in sight of the house. I rode up to Uncle Buck. 'Give me the pistol,' I said.

'We ain't going to need a pistol,' Uncle Buck said. 'He ain't even here, I tell you. You and that nigger stay back and let me do this. I'm going to find out which a way to start hunting. Get back, now.'

'No,' I said, 'I want –'

He looked at me from under the crokersack. 'You want what? You want to lay your two hands on the man that shot Rosa Millard, don't you?' He looked at me. I sat there on the mule in the slow grey cold rain, in the dying daylight. Maybe it was the cold. I didn't feel cold, but I could feel my bones jerking and shaking. 'And then what you going to do with him?' Uncle Buck said. He was almost whispering now. 'Hey? Hey?'

'Yes,' I said. 'Yes.'

'Yes. That's what. Now you and Ringo stay back. I'll do this.'

It was just a cabin. I reckon there were a thousand of them just like it about our hills, with the same canted plough lying under a tree and the same bedraggled chickens roosting on the plough and the same grey twilight dissolving on to the grey shingles of the roof. Then we saw a faint crack of fire and a woman's face looking at us around the crack of the door.

'Mr Snopes ain't here, if that's what you want,' she said. 'He's done gone to Alabama on a visit.'

'Sho, now,' Uncle Buck said. 'To Alabama. Did he leave any word when to expect him home?'

'No,' the woman said.

'Sho, now,' Uncle Buck said. 'Then I reckon we better get on back home and out of the rain.'

'I reckon you had,' the woman said. Then the door closed.

We rode away. We rode back towards home. It was like it had been while we waited at the old compress; it hadn't got darker exactly, the twilight had just thickened.

'Well, well, well,' Uncle Buck said. 'They ain't in Alabama, because she told us so. And they ain't towards Memphis, because there are still Yankees there yet. So I reckon we better try down towards Grenada first. By Godfrey, I'll bet this mule against that nigger's pocket knife that we won't ride two days before we come on a mad woman hollering down the road with a handful of chicken feathers in her hand. You come on here and listen to me. By Godfrey, we're going to do this thing but by Godfrey we're going to do it right.'

2

So we didn't get Ab Snopes that day. We didn't get him for a lot of days, and nights too – days in which we rode, the three of us, on relays of Granny's and Ringo's Yankee mules along the known roads and the unknown (and sometimes unmarked) trails and paths, in the wet and the iron frost, and nights when we slept in the same wet and the same freeze and (once) in the snow, beneath whatever shelter we found when night found us. They had neither name nor number. They lasted from that December afternoon until late February, until one night we realized that we had been hearing geese and ducks going north for some time. At first Ringo kept a pine stick and each night he would cut a notch in it, with a big one for Sunday and two long ones which meant Christmas and New Year's. But one night when the stick had almost forty notches in it, we stopped in the rain to make camp without any roof to get under and we had to use the stick to start a fire, because of Uncle Buck's arm. And so, when we came to where we could get another pine stick, we couldn't remember whether it had been five or six or ten days, and so Ringo didn't start another. Because he said he would fix the stick up the day we got Grumby and that it wouldn't need but two notches on it – one for the day we got him and one for the day Granny died.

We had two mules apiece, to swap on to at noon each day.

We got the mules back from the hill people; we could have got a cavalry regiment if we had wanted it – of old men and women and children, too – with cotton bagging and flour sacking for uniforms and hoes and axes for arms, on the Yankee mules that Granny had loaned to them. But Uncle Buck told them that we didn't need any help; that three was enough to catch Grumby.

They were not hard to follow. One day we had about twenty notches on the stick and we came on to a house where the ashes were still smoking and a boy almost as big as Ringo and me still unconscious in the stable with even his shirt cut to pieces like they had had a wire snapper on the whip, and a woman with a little thread of blood still running out of her mouth and her voice sounding light and far away like a locust from across the pasture, telling us how many there were and which way they would likely go saying, 'Kill them. Kill them.'

It was a long way, but it wasn't far. You could have put a silver dollar down on the geography page with the centre of it at Jefferson and we would have never ridden out from under it. And we were closer behind them than we knew, because one night we had ridden late without coming to a house or a shed to camp in, and so we stopped and Ringo said he would scout around a little, because all we had left to eat was the bone of a ham; only it was more likely Ringo was trying to dodge helping to get in the firewood. So Uncle Buck and I were spreading down pine branches to sleep on when we heard a shot and then a sound like a brick chimney falling on to a rotten shingle roof, and then the horses, starting fast and dying away, and then I could hear Ringo yelling. He had come on to a house; he thought it was deserted, and then he said it looked too dark, too quiet. So he climbed on to a shed against the back wall, and he said he saw the crack of light and he was trying to pull the shutter open careful, but it came loose with a sound like a shot, and he was looking into a room with a candle stuck into a bottle and either three or thirteen men looking right at him; and how somebody hollered, 'There they are!' and another man jerked out a pistol and one of the others grabbed his arm as it went off, and then the whole shed gave way under him, and he said how he lay there hollering and trying to get untangled from the broken planks and heard them ride away.

'So he didn't shoot at you,' Uncle Buck said.

'Hit warn't none of his fault if he never,' Ringo said.

'But he didn't,' Uncle Buck said. But he wouldn't let us go on that night. 'We won't lose any distance,' he said. 'They are flesh and blood, the same as we are. And we ain't scared.'

So we went on at daylight, following the hoofprints now. Then we had three more notches in the stick; that night Ringo put the last notch in it that he was going to, but we didn't know it. We were sitting in front of a cotton pen where we were going to sleep, eating a shote that Ringo had found, when we heard the horse. Then the man begun to holler, 'Hello! Hello?' and then we watch him ride up on a good short-coupled sorrel mare, with his neat little fine-made boots, and his linen shirt without any collar, and a coat that had been good, too, once, and a broad hat pulled down so that all we could see was his eyes and nose between the hat and his black beard.

'Howdy, men,' he said.

'Howdy,' Uncle Buck said. He was eating a sparerib; he sat now with the rib in his left hand and his right hand lying on his lap just inside his coat; he wore the pistol on a loop of lace leather around his neck and stuck into his pants like a lady's watch. But the stranger wasn't looking at him; he just looked at each of us once and then sat there on the mare, with both his hands on the pommel in front of him.

'Mind if I light and warm?' he said.

'Light,' Uncle Buck said.

He got off. But he didn't hitch the mare. He led her up and he sat down opposite us with the reins in his hand. 'Give the stranger some meat, Ringo,' Uncle Buck said. But he didn't take it. He didn't move. He just said that he had eaten, sitting there on the log with his little feet side by side and his elbows out a little and his two hands on his knees as small as a woman's hands and covered with a light mat of fine black hair right down to the finger nails, and not looking at any of us now. I don't know what he was looking at now.

'I have just ridden out from Memphis,' he said. 'How far do you call it to Alabama?'

Uncle Buck told him, not moving either, with the sparerib

still raised in his left hand and the other hand lying just inside his coat. 'You going to Alabama, hey?'

'Yes,' the stranger said. 'I'm looking for a man.' And now I saw that he was looking at me from under his hat. 'A man named Grumby. You people in these parts may have heard of him too.'

'Yes,' Uncle Buck said, 'we have heard of him.'

'Ah,' the stranger said. He smiled; for a second his teeth looked white as rice inside his ink-coloured beard. 'Then what I am doing does not have to be secret.' He looked at Uncle Buck now. 'I live up in Tennessee. Grumby and his gang killed one of my niggers and ran my horses off. I'm going to get the horses back. If I have to take Grumby in the bargain, that will suit me too.'

'Sho, now,' Uncle Buck said. 'So you look to find him in Alabama?'

'Yes. I happen to know that he is now headed there. I almost caught him yesterday; I did get one of his men, though the others escaped me. They passed you all sometime last night, if you were in this neighbourhood then. You would have heard them, because when I last saw them, they were not wasting any time. I managed to persuade the man I caught to tell me where they are to rondyvoo.'

'Alabama?' Ringo said. 'You mean they headed back towards Alabama?'

'Correct,' the stranger said. He looked at Ringo now, 'Did Grumby steal your hog, too, boy?'

'Hawg,' Ringo said. 'Hawg?'

'Put some wood on the fire,' Uncle Buck told Ringo. 'Save your breath to snore with tonight.'

Ringo hushed, but he didn't move; he sat there staring back at the stranger, with his eyes looking a little red in the firelight.

'So you folks are out to catch a man, too, are you?' the stranger said.

'Two is correct,' Ringo said. 'I reckon Ab Snopes can pass for a man.'

So then it was too late; we just sat there, with the stranger facing us across the fire with the mare's reins in his little still hand, looking at the three of us from between his hat and his beard. 'Ab Snopes,' he said. 'I don't believe I am acquainted with Ab Snopes. But I know Grumby. And you want Grumby too.' He was looking at all of us now. 'You want to catch Grumby. Don't you think that's dangerous?'

'Not exactly,' Uncle Buck said. 'You see, we done got a little Alabama Grumby evidence ourselves. That something or somebody has give Grumby a change of heart about killing women and children.' He and the stranger looked at each other. 'Maybe it's the wrong season for women and children. Or maybe it's public opinion, now that Grumby is what you might call a public character. Folks hereabouts is got used to having their menfolks killed and even shot from behind. But even the Yankees never got them used to the other. And evidently somebody has done reminded Grumby of this. Ain't that correct?'

They looked at each other; they didn't move. 'But you are neither a woman nor a child, old man,' the stranger said. He stood up, easy; his eyes glinted in the firelight as he turned and put the reins over the mare's head. 'I reckon I'll get along,' he said. We watched him get into the saddle and sit there again, with his little black-haired hands lying on the pommel, looking down at us – at me and Ringo now. 'So you want Ab Snopes,' he said. 'Take a stranger's advice and stick to him.'

He turned the mare. I was watching him, then I was thinking 'I wonder if he knows that her off back shoe is gone,' when Ringo hollered, 'Look out!' and then it seemed to me that I saw the spurred mare jump before I saw the pistol flash; and then the mare was galloping and Uncle Buck was lying on the ground cussing and yelling and dragging at his pistol, and then all three of us were dragging and fighting over it, but the front sight was caught in his suspenders, and the three of us fighting over it, and Uncle Buck panting and cussing, and the sound of the galloping mare dying away.

The bullet went through the flesh of the inner side of the arm that had the rheumatism; that was why Uncle Buck cussed so bad; he said the rheumatism was bad enough, and the bullet was bad enough, but to have them both at once was too much for any man. And then, when Ringo told him he ought to be thankful, that suppose the bullet had hit his good arm and then he wouldn't even be able to feed himself, he reached back and, still lying down, he caught up a stick of firewood and tried to hit Ringo with it. We cut his sleeve away and stopped the blood, and he made me cut a strip off his shirt tail, and Ringo handed him his stick and he sat there cussing us while we soaked the strip in hot salt water, and he held the arm himself with his good hand, cussing a steady streak, and made us run the strip back and forth through the hole the bullet had made. He cussed then sure enough, looking a little like Granny looked, like all old people look when they have been hurt, with his beard jerking and his eyes snapping and his heels and the stick jabbing into the ground like the stick had been with him so long that it felt the rag and the salt too.

And at first I thought that the black man was Grumby, like I had thought that maybe Ab Snopes was. But Uncle Buck said not. It was the next morning; we hadn't slept much because Uncle Buck wouldn't go to sleep; only we didn't know then that it was his arm, because he wouldn't even let us talk about taking him back home. And now we tried again, after we had finished breakfast, but he wouldn't listen, already on his mule with his left arm tied across his chest and the pistol stuck between the arm and his chest, where he could get to it quick, saying, 'Wait. Wait,' and his eyes hard and snapping with thinking. 'It's something I ain't quite got yet,' he said. 'Something he was telling us last night without aiming to have us know yet that he had told us. Something that we are going to find out today.'

'Likely a bullet that's fixing to hit you half-way betwixt both arms stid of half-way betwixt one,' Ringo said.

Uncle Buck rode fast; we could watch his stick rising and falling against the mule's flank, not hard, just steady and fast, like a crippled man in a hurry that has used the stick so long he don't even know it any more. Because we didn't know that his arm was making him sick yet; he hadn't given us time to realize it. So we hurried on, riding along beside a slough, and then Ringo saw the snake. It had been warm for a week, until last night. But last night it made ice, and now we saw the moccasin where it had crawled out and was trying to get back into the water when the cold got it, so that it lay with its body on the land and its head fixed in the skim ice like it was set into a mirror, and Uncle Buck turned sideways on his mule, hollering at us: 'There it is, by Godfrey! There's the sign! Didn't I tell you we would –'

We all heard it at once – the three or maybe four shots and then the sound of horses galloping, except that some of the galloping came from Uncle Buck's mule, and he had his pistol out now before he turned from the road and into the trees, with the stick jammed under his hurt arm and his beard flying back over his shoulder. But we didn't find anything. We saw the marks in the mud where the five horses had stood while the men that rode them had watched the road, and we saw the sliding tracks where the horses had begun to gallop, and I thinking quietly, 'He still don't know that that shoe is gone.' But that was all, and Uncle Buck sitting on his mule with the pistol raised in his hand and his beard blown back over his shoulder and the leather thong of the pistol hanging down his back like a girl's pigtail, and his mouth open and his eyes blinking at me and Ringo.

'What in the tarnation hell!' he said. 'Well, let's go back to the road. Whatever it was has done gone that way too.'

So we had turned. Uncle Buck had put the pistol up and his stick had begun to beat the mule again when we saw what it was, what it meant.

It was Ab Snopes. He was lying on his side, tied hand and foot, and hitched to a sapling; we could see the marks in the mud where he had tried to roll back into the underbrush until the rope stopped him. He had been watching us all the time, lying there with his face in the shape of snarling and not making a sound after he found out he could not roll out of sight. He was watching our mules' legs and feet under the bushes; he hadn't thought to look any higher yet, and so he did not know that we could see him; he must have thought that we had just spied him, because all of a sudden he began to jerk and thrash on the ground, hollering, 'Help! Help! Help!'

We untied him and got him on to his feet, and he was still hollering, loud, with his face and his arms jerking, about how they had caught and robbed him, and they would have killed him if they hadn't heard us coming and run away; only his eyes were not hollering. They were watching us, going fast and quick from Ringo to me to Uncle Buck, and then at Ringo and me again, and they were not hollering, like his eyes belonged to one man and his gaped and yelling mouth belonged to another.

'So they caught you, hey?' Uncle Buck said. 'A innocent and unsuspecting traveller. I reckon the name of them would never be Grumby now, would it?'

It was like we might have stopped and built a fire and thawed out that moccasin – just enough for it to find out where it was, but not enough for it to know what to do about it. Only I reckon it was a high compliment to set Ab Snopes up with a moccasin, even a little one. I reckon it was bad for him. I reckon he realized that they had thrown him back to us without mercy, and that if he tried to save himself from us at their expense, they would come back and kill him. I reckon he decided that the worst thing that could happen to him would be for us not to do anything to him at all. Because he quit jerking his arms; he even quit lying; for a minute his eyes and his mouth were telling the same thing.

'I made a mistake,' he said. 'I admit hit. I reckon everybody does. The question is, what are you fellows going to do about hit?'

'Yes,' Uncle Buck said. 'Everybody makes mistakes. Your trouble is, you make too many. Because mistakes are bad. Look at Rosa Millard. She just made one, and look at her. And you have made two.'

Ab Snopes watched Uncle Buck. 'What's them?'

'Being born too soon and dying too late,' Uncle Buck said.

He looked at all of us, fast; he didn't move, still talking to Uncle Buck. 'You ain't going to kill me. You don't dast.'

'I don't even need to,' Uncle Buck said. 'It wasn't my grand-maw you sicked on to that snake den.'

He looked at me now, but his eyes were going again, back and forth across me at Ringo and Uncle Buck; it was the two of them again now, the eyes and the voice. 'Why, then I'm all right. Bayard ain't got no hard feelings against me. He knows hit was a pure accident; that we was doing hit for his sake and his paw and them niggers at home. Why, here hit's a whole year and it was me that holp and tended Miss Rosa when she never had ara living soul but them chil – ' Now the voice began to tell the truth again; it was the eyes and the voice that I was walking towards. He fell back, crouching, his hands flung up.

Behind me, Uncle Buck said, 'You, Ringo! Stay back.'

He was walking backward now, with his hands flung up, hollering. 'Three on one! Three on one!'

'Stand still,' Uncle Buck said. 'Ain't no three on you. I don't see nobody on you but one of them children you was just mentioning.' Then we were both down in the mud; and then I couldn't see him, and I couldn't seem to find him any more, not even with the hollering; and then I was fighting three or four for a long time before Uncle Buck and Ringo held me, and then I could see him again, lying on the ground with his arms over his face. 'Get up,' Uncle Buck said.

'No,' he said. 'Three of you can jump on me and knock me down again, but you got to pick me up first to do hit. I ain't got no rights and justice here, but you can't keep me from protesting hit.'

'Lift him up,' Uncle Buck said. 'I'll hold Bayard.'

Ringo lifted him; it was like lifting up a half-filled cotton sack. 'Stand up, Mr Ab Snopes,' Ringo said. But he would not stand, not even after Ringo and Uncle Buck tied him to the sapling and Ringo had taken off his and Uncle Buck's and Ab Snopes' galluses and knotted them together with the bridle reins from the mules. He just hung there in the rope, not even flinching when the lash fell, saying, 'That's hit. Whup me. Lay hit on me; you got me three to one.'

'Wait,' Uncle Buck said. Ringo stopped. 'You want another chance with one to one? You can take your choice of the three of us.'

'I got my rights,' he said. 'I'm helpless, but I can still protest hit. Whup me.'

I reckon he was right. I reckon if we had let him go clean, they would have circled back and killed him themselves before dark. Because – that was the night it began to rain and we had to burn Ringo's stick because Uncle Buck admitted now that his arm was getting bad – we all ate supper together, and it was Ab Snopes that was the most anxious about Uncle Buck, saying how it wasn't any hard feelings and that he could see himself that he had made a mistake in trusting the folks he did, and that all he wanted to do now was to go back home, because it was only the folks you had known all your life that you could trust, and when you put faith in a stranger you deserved what you got when you found that what you had been eating and sleeping with was no better than a passel of rattlesnakes, But as soon as Uncle Buck tried to find out if it actually was Grumby, he shut up and denied that he had ever seen him.

They left us early the next morning. Uncle Buck was sick by then; we offered to ride back home with him, or to let Ringo ride back with him, and I would keep Ab Snopes with me, but Uncle Buck wouldn't have it.

'Grumby might capture him again and tie him to another sapling in the road, and you would lose time burying him,' Uncle Buck said. 'You boys go on. It ain't going to be long now. And catch them!' He began to holler, with his face flushed and his eyes bright, taking the pistol from around his neck and giving it to me, 'Catch them! Catch them!'

3

So Ringo and I went on. It rained all that day; now it began to rain all the time. We had the two mules apiece; we went fast. It rained; sometimes we had no fire at all; that was when we lost count of time, because one morning we came to a fire still burning and a hog they had not even had time to butcher; and sometimes we would ride all night, swapping mules when we had guessed that it had been two hours; and so, sometimes it would be night when we slept and sometimes it would be daylight, and we knew that they must have watched us from somewhere every day and that now that Uncle Buck was not with us, they didn't even dare to stop and try to hide.

Then one afternoon – the rain had stopped but the clouds had not broken and it was turning cold again – it was about dusk and we were galloping along an old road in the river bottom; it was dim and narrow under the trees and we were galloping when my mule shied and swerved and stopped, and I just did catch myself before I went over his head; and then we saw the thing hanging over the middle of the road from a limb. It was an old Negro man, with a rim of white hair and with his bare toes pointing down and his head on one side like he was thinking about something quiet. The note was pinned to him, but we couldn't read it until we rode on into a clearing. It was a scrap of dirty paper with big crude printed letters, like a child might have made them:

Last woning not thret. Turn back. The barer of this my promise and garntee. I have stood all I aim to stand children no children. G

And something else written beneath it in a hand neat and small and prettier than Granny's, only you knew that a man had written it; and while I looked at the dirty paper I could see him again, with his neat little feet and his little black-haired hands and his fine soiled shirt and his fine muddy coat, across the fire from us that night.

This is signed by others beside G., one of wh^m in particular hav^{ng} less scruples re children than he has. Nethless unders^{gnd} desires to give both you and G. one more chance. Take it and some day become a man. Refuse it, and cease even to be a child.

Ringo and I looked at each other. There had been a house here once, but it was gone now. Beyond the clearing the road went on again into the thick trees in the grey twilight. 'Maybe it will be tomorrow,' Ringo said.

It was tomorrow; we slept that night in a haystack, but we were riding again by daylight, following the dim road along the river bottom. This time it was Ringo's mule that shied; the man had stepped out of the bushes that quick, with his fine muddy boots and coat and the pistol in his little black-haired hand, and only his eyes and his nose showing between his hat and his beard.

'Stay where you are,' he said. 'I will still be watching you.'

We didn't move. We watched him step back into the bushes, then the three of them came out – the bearded man and another man walking abreast and leading two saddled horses, and the third man walking just in front of them with his hands behind him – a thick-built man with a reddish stubble and pale eyes, in a faded Confederate uniform coat and Yankee boots, bare-headed, with a long smear of dried blood on his cheek and one side of his coat caked with dried mud and that sleeve ripped away at the shoulder, but we didn't realize at once that what made his shoulders look so thick was that his arms were tied tight behind him. And then all of a sudden we knew that at last we were looking at Grumby. We knew it long before the bearded man said, 'You want Grumby. Here he is.'

We just sat there. Because from then on, the other two men did not even look at us again. 'I'll take him now,' the bearded man said. 'Get on your horse.' The other man got on one of the horses. We could see the pistol in his hand then, pointed at Grumby's back. 'Hand me your knife,' the bearded man said.

Without moving the pistol, the other man passed his knife to the bearded man. Then Grumby spoke; he had not moved until now; he just stood there with his shoulders hunched and his little pale eyes blinking at me and Ringo.

'Boys,' he said, 'boys – '

'Shut your mouth,' the bearded man said, in a cold, quiet, almost pleasant voice. 'You've already talked too much. If you had done what I wanted done that night in December, you wouldn't be where you are now.' We saw his hand with the knife; I reckon maybe for a minute Ringo and I and Grumby, too, all thought the same thing. But he just cut Grumby's hands loose and stepped back quick. But when Grumby turned, he turned right into the pistol in the bearded man's hand.

'Steady,' the bearded man said. 'Have you got him, Bridger?'

'Yes,' the other man said. The bearded man backed to the other horse and got on it without lowering his pistol or ceasing to watch Grumby. Then he sat there, too, looking down at Grumby, with his little hooked nose and his eyes alone showing between the hat and the ink-coloured beard. Grumby began to move his head from side to side.

'Boys,' he said, 'boys, you ain't going to do this to me.'

'We're not going to do anything to you,' the bearded man said. 'I can't speak for these boys there. But since you are so delicate about children, maybe they will be delicate with you. But we'll give you a chance though.' His other hand went inside his coat too fast to watch; it had hardly disappeared before the other pistol flicked out and turned once and fell at Grumby's feet; again Grumby moved, but the pistols stopped him. The bearded man sat easy on the horse, looking down at Grumby, talking in that cold, still, vicious voice that wasn't even mad:

'We had a good thing in this country. We would have it yet, if it hadn't been for you. And now we've got to pull out. Got to leave it because you lost your nerve and killed an old woman and then lost your nerve again and refused to cover the first mistake. Scruples,' he said. 'Scruples. So afraid of raising the country that there ain't a man, woman or child, black or white, in it that ain't on the watch for us. And all because you got scared and killed an old woman you never saw before. Not to get anything; not for one single Confed bank-note. But because you got scared of a piece of paper on which someone had signed Bedford Forrest's name. And you with one exactly like it in your pocket now.'

He didn't look at the other man, Bridger; he just said, 'All right. Ease off. But watch him. He's too tender-hearted to turn your back on.'

They backed the horses away, side by side, the two pistols trained on Grumby's belly, until they reached the underbrush. 'We're going to Texas. If you should leave this place, I would advise you to go at least that far also. But just remember that Texas is a wide place, and use that knowledge. Ride!' he shouted.

He whirled the mare. Bridger whirled too. As they did so, Grumby leaped and caught the pistol from the ground and ran forward, crouching and shouting into the bushes, cursing. He shot three times towards the fading sound of the horses, then he whirled back to face us. Ringo and I were on the ground, too; I don't remember when we got down nor why, but we were down, and I remember how I looked once at Ringo's face and then how I stood there with Uncle Buck's pistol feeling heavy as a firedog in my hand. Then I saw that he had quit whirling; that he was standing there with the pistol hanging against his right leg and that he was looking at me; and then all of a sudden he was smiling.

'Well, boys,' he said, 'it looks like you have got me. Durn my hide for letting Matt Bowden fool me into emptying my pistol at him.'

And I could hear my voice; it sounded faint and far away,

like the woman's in Alabama that day, so that I wondered if he could hear me: 'You shot three times. You have got two more shots in it.'

His face didn't change, or I couldn't see it change. It just lowered, looking down, but the smile was gone from it. 'In this pistol?' he said. It was like he was examining a pistol for the first time, so slow and careful it was that he passed it from his right to his left hand and let it hang again, pointing down again. 'Well, well, well. Sholy I ain't forgot how to count as well as how to shoot.' There was a bird somewhere – a yellow-hammer – I had been hearing it all the time; even the three shots hadn't frightened it. And I could hear Ringo, too, making a kind of whimpering sound when he breathed, and it was like I wasn't trying to watch Grumby so much as to keep from look-ing at Ringo. 'Well, she's safe enough now, since it don't look like I can even shoot with my right hand.'

Then it happened. I know what did happen, but even now I don't know how, in what order. Because he was big and squat, like a bear. But when we had first seen him he was a captive, and so, even now he seemed more like a stump than even an animal, even though we had watched him leap and catch up the pistol and run firing after the other two. All I know is, one second he was standing there in his muddy Confederate coat, smiling at us, with his ragged teeth showing a little in his red stubble, with the thin sunlight on the stubble and on his shoulders and cuffs, on the dark marks where the braid had been ripped away; and the next second there were two bright orange splashes, one after the other, against the middle of the grey coat and the coat itself swelling slow down on me like when Granny told us about the balloon she saw in St Louis and we would dream about it.

I reckon I heard the sound, and I reckon I must have heard the bullets, and I reckon I felt him when he hit me, but I don't remember it. I just remember the two bright flashes and the grey coat rushing down, and then the ground hitting me. But I could smell him – the smell of man sweat, and the grey coat grinding into my face and smelling of horse sweat and wood smoke and grease – and I could hear him, and then I could hear my arm socket, and I thought 'In a minute I will hear my fingers breaking, but I have got to hold on to it' and then – I don't know whether it was under or over his arm or his leg – I saw Ringo, in the air, looking exactly like a frog, even to the eyes, with his mouth open too and his open pocket knife in his hand.

Then I was free. I saw Ringo straddle of Grumby's back and Grumby getting up from his hands and knees and I tried to raise the pistol only my arm wouldn't move. Then Grumby bucked Ringo off just like a steer would and whirled again, looking at us, crouched, with his mouth open too; and then my arm began to come up with the pistol and he turned and ran. He shouldn't have tried to run from us in boots. Or maybe that made no difference either, because now my arm had come up and now I could see Grumby's back (he didn't scream, he never made a sound) and the pistol both at the same time and the pistol was level and steady as a rock.

4

It took us the rest of that day and part of the night to reach the old compress. But it didn't take very long to ride home because we went fast with the two mounts apiece to change to, and what we had to carry now, wrapped in a piece of the skirt of Grumby's coat, didn't weigh anything.

It was almost dark when we rode through Jefferson; it was raining again when we rode past the brick piles and the sooty walls that hadn't fallen down yet, and went on through what used to be the square. We hitched the mules in the cedars and Ringo was just starting off to find a board when we saw that somebody had already put one up – Mrs Compson, I reckon, or maybe Uncle Buck when he got back home. We already had the piece of wire.

The earth had sunk too now, after two months; it was almost level now, like at first Granny had not wanted to be dead either but now she had begun to be reconciled. We unwrapped it from the jagged square of stained faded grey cloth and fastened it to the board. 'Now she can lay good and quiet,' Ringo said.

'Yes,' I said. And then we both began to cry. We stood there in the slow rain, crying. We had ridden a lot, and during the last week we hadn't slept much and we hadn't always had anything to eat.

'It wasn't him or Ab Snopes either that kilt her,' Ringo said. 'It was them mules. That first batch of mules we got for nothing.'

'Yes,' I said. 'Let's go home. I reckon Louvinia is worried about us.'

So it was good and dark when we came to the cabin. And then we saw that it was lighted like for Christmas; we could see the big fire and the lamp, clean and bright, when Louvinia opened the door long before we had got to it and ran out into the rain and began to paw at me, crying and hollering.

'What?' I said. 'Father? Father's home? Father?'

'And Miss Drusilla!' Louvinia hollered, crying and praying and pawing at me, and hollering and scolding at Ringo all at once. 'Home! Hit done finished! All but the surrendering. And now Marse John done home.' She finally told us how Father and Drusilla had come home about a week ago and Uncle Buck told Father where Ringo and I were, and how Father had tried to make Drusilla wait at home, but she refused, and how they were looking for us, with Uncle Buck to show the way.

So we went to bed. We couldn't even stay awake to eat the supper Louvinia cooked for us; Ringo and I went to bed in our clothes on the pallet, and went to sleep all in one motion, with Louvinia's face hanging over us and still scolding, and Joby in the chimney corner where Louvinia had made him get up out of Granny's chair. And then somebody was pulling at me, and I thought I was fighting Ab Snopes again, and then it was the rain in Father's beard and clothes that I smelled. But Uncle Buck was still hollering, and Father holding me, and Ringo and I held to him, and then it was Drusilla kneeling and holding me and Ringo, and we could smell the rain in her hair, too, while she was hollering at Uncle Buck to hush. Father's hand was hard; I could see his face beyond Drusilla and I was trying to say, 'Father, Father,' while she was holding me and Ringo with the rain smell of her hair all round us, and Uncle Buck hollering and Joby looking at Uncle Buck with his mouth open and his eyes round.

'Yes, by Godfrey! Not only tracked him down and caught

him but brought back the actual proof of it to where Rosa Millard could rest quiet.'

'The which?' Joby hollered. 'Fotch back the which?'

'Hush! Hush!' Drusilla said. 'That's all done, all finished. You, Uncle Buck!'

'The proof and the expiation!' Uncle Buck hollered. 'When me and John Sartoris and Drusilla rode up to that old compress, the first thing we see was that murdering scoundrel pegged out on the door to it like a coon hide, all except the right hand. "And if anybody wants to see that, too," I told John Sartoris, "just let them ride into Jefferson and look on Rosa Millard's grave!" Ain't I told you he is John Sartoris' boy? Hey? Ain't I told you?'

Skirmish at Sartoris

I

When I think of that day, of Father's old troop on their horses drawn up facing the house, and Father and Drusilla on the ground with that Carpet Bagger voting box in front of them, and opposite them the women – Aunt Louisa, Mrs Habersham and all the others – on the porch and the two sets of them, the men and the women, facing one another like they were both waiting for a bugle to sound the charge, I think I know the reason. I think it was because Father's troop (like all the other Southern soldiers too), even though they had surrendered and said that they were whipped, were still soldiers. Maybe from the old habit of doing everything as one man; maybe when you have lived for four years in a world ordered completely by men's doings, even when it is danger and fighting, you don't want to quit that world: maybe the danger and the fighting are the reasons, because men have been pacifists for every reason under the sun except to avoid danger and fighting. And so now Father's troop and all the other men in Jefferson, and Aunt Louisa and Mrs Habersham and all the women in Jefferson were actually enemies for the reason that the men had given in and admitted that they belonged to the United States but the women had never surrendered.

I remember the night we got the letter and found out at last where Drusilla was. It was just before Christmas in 1864, after the Yankees had burned Jefferson and gone away, and we didn't even know for sure if the war was still going on or not. All we knew was that for three years the country had been full of Yankees, and then all of a sudden they were gone and there were no men there at all any more. We hadn't even heard from Father since July, from Carolina, so that now we lived in a world of burned towns and houses and ruined plantations and fields inhabited only by women. Ringo and I were fifteen then; we felt almost exactly like we had to eat and sleep and change our clothes in a hotel built only for ladies and children.

The envelope was worn and dirty and it had been opened

once and then glued back, but we could still make out *Hawk-hurst, Gihon County, Alabama* on it even though we did not recognize Aunt Louisa's hand at first. It was addressed to Granny; it was six pages cut with scissors from wallpaper and written on both sides with pokeberry juice and I thought of that night eighteen months ago when Drusilla and I stood outside the cabin at Hawkhurst and listened to the niggers passing in the road, the night when she told me about the dog, about keeping the dog quiet, and then asked me to ask Father to let her join his troop and ride with him. But I didn't tell Father. Maybe I forgot it. Then the Yankees went away and Father and his troop went away too. Then, six months later, we had a letter from him about how they were fighting in Carolina, and a month after that we had one from Aunt Louisa that Drusilla was gone too, a short letter on the wallpaper that you could see where Aunt Louisa had cried in the pokeberry juice about how she did not know where Drusilla was but that she had expected the worst ever since Drusilla had deliberately tried to unsex herself by refusing to feel any natural grief at the death in battle not only of her affianced husband but of her own father and that she took it for granted that Drusilla was with us and though she did not expect Drusilla to take any steps herself to relieve a mother's anxiety, she hoped that Granny would. But we didn't know where Drusilla was either. She had just vanished. It was like the Yankees in just passing through the South had not only taken along with them all living men blue and grey and white and black, but even one young girl who had happened to try to look and act like a man after her sweetheart was killed.

So then the next letter came. Only Granny wasn't there to read it because she was dead then (it was the time when Grumby doubled back past Jefferson and so Ringo and I spent one night at home and found the letter when Mrs Compson had sent it out) and so for a while Ringo and I couldn't make out what Aunt Louisa was trying to tell us. This one was on the same wallpaper too, six pages this time, only Aunt Louisa hadn't cried in the pokeberry juice this time: Ringo said because she must have been writing too fast:

Dear Sister:

I think this will be news to you as it was to me though I both hope and pray it will not be the heartrending shock to you it was to me as naturally it cannot since you are only an aunt while I am the mother. But it is not myself I am thinking of since I am a woman, a mother, a Southern woman, and it has been our lot during the last four years to learn to bear anything. But when I think of my husband who laid down his life to protect a heritage of courageous men and spotless women looking down from heaven upon a daughter who had deliberately cast away that for which he died, and when I think of my half-orphan son who will one day ask of me why his martyred father's sacrifice was not enough to preserve his sister's good name –

That's how it sounded. Ringo was holding a pineknot for me to read by, but after a while he had to light another pineknot and all the farther we had got was how when Gavin Breckbridge was killed at Shiloh before he and Drusilla had had time to marry, there had been reserved for Drusilla the highest destiny of a Southern woman – to be the bride-widow of a lost cause – and how Drusilla had not only thrown that away, she had not only become a lost woman and a shame to her father's memory but she was now living in a word that Aunt Louisa would not even repeat but that Granny knew what it was, though at least thank God that Father and Drusilla were not actually any blood kin, it being Father's wife who was Drusilla's cousin by blood and not Father himself. So then Ringo lit the other pineknot and then we put the sheets of wallpaper down on the floor and then we found out what it was: how Drusilla had been gone for six months and no word from her except she was alive, and then one night she walked into the cabin where Aunt Louisa and Denny were (and now it had a line drawn under it) *in the garments not alone of a man but of a common private soldier* and told them how she had been a member of Father's troop for six months, bivouacking at night surrounded by sleeping men and not even bothering to put up the tent for her and Father except when the weather was bad, and how Drusilla not only showed neither shame nor remorse but actually pretended she did not even know what Aunt Louisa was talking about; how when Aunt Louisa told her that she and Father must marry at once, Drusilla said, 'Can't you understand that I am tired of burying husbands in this war? That I am riding in Cousin John's troop not to find a man but to hurt Yankees?' and how Aunt Louisa said:

'At least don't call him *Cousin* John where strangers can hear you.'

2

The third letter did not come to us at all. It came to Mrs Compson. Drusilla and Father were home then. It was in the spring and the war was over now, and we were busy getting the cypress and oak out of the bottom to build the house and Drusilla working with Joby and Ringo and Father and me like another man, with her hair shorter than it had been at Hawkhurst and her face sunburned from riding in the weather and her body thin from living like soldiers lived. After Granny died Ringo and Louvinia and I all slept in the cabin, but after Father came Ringo and Louvinia moved back to the other cabin with Joby and now Father and I slept on Ringo's and my pallet and Drusilla slept in the bed behind the quilt curtain where Granny used to sleep. And so one night I remembered Aunt Louisa's letter and I showed it to Drusilla and Father, and Father found out that Drusilla had not written to tell Aunt Louisa where she was and Father said she must, and so one day Mrs Compson came out with the third letter. Drusilla and Ringo and Louvinia too were down in the bottom at the sawmill and I saw that one too, on the wallpaper with the pokeberry juice and the juice not cried on this time either, and this the first time Mrs Compson had come out since Granny died and not even getting out of her surrey but sitting there holding to her parasol with one hand and her shawl with the other and looking round like when Drusilla would come out of the house or from round the corner it would not be just a thin sunburned girl in a man's shirt and pants but maybe something like a tame panther or bear. This one sounded just like the others: about how Aunt Louisa was addressing a stranger to herself but not a stranger to Granny and that there were times when the good name of one family was the good name of all and that she naturally did not expect Mrs Compson to move out and live with Father and Drusilla because even that would be too late now to preserve the appearance of that which had never existed anyway. But that Mrs Compson was a woman too, Aunt Louisa believed, a Southern

woman too, and had suffered too, Aunt Louisa didn't doubt,
only she did hope and pray that Mrs Compson had been spared
the sight of her own daughter if Mrs Compson had one flouting
and outraging all Southern principles of purity and woman-
hood that our husbands had died for, though Aunt Louisa
hoped again that Mrs Compson's husband (Mrs Compson was
a good deal older than Granny and the only husband she had
ever had had been locked up for crazy a long time ago because
in the slack part of the afternoons he would gather up eight or
ten little niggers from the quarters and line them up across the
creek from him with sweet potatoes on their heads and he would
shoot the potatoes off with a rifle; he would tell them he might
miss a potato but he wasn't going to miss a nigger, and so they
would stand mighty still) had not made one of the number. So
I couldn't make any sense out of that one too and I still didn't
know what Aunt Louisa was talking about and I didn't believe
that Mrs Compson knew either.

Because it was not her: it was Mrs Habersham, that never
had been out here before and that Granny never had been to see
that I knew of. Because Mrs Compson didn't stay, she didn't
even get out of the surrey, sitting there kind of drawn up under
the shawl and looking at me and then at the cabin like she didn't
know just what might come out of it or out from behind it.
Then she began to tap the nigger driver on his head with the
parasol and they went away, the two old horses going pretty
fast back down the drive and back down the road to town. And
the next afternoon when I came out of the bottom to go to the
spring with the water bucket there were five surreys and
buggies in front of the cabin and inside the cabin there were
fourteen of them that had come the four miles out from Jefferson, in the Sunday clothes that the Yankees and the war had
left them, that had husbands dead in the war or alive back in
Jefferson helping Father with what he was doing, because they
were strange times then. Only like I said, maybe times are never
strange to women: that it is just one continuous monotonous
thing full of the repeated follies of their menfolks. Mrs Compson was sitting in Granny's chair, still holding the parasol and
drawn up under her shawl and looking like she had finally seen
whatever it was she had expected to see, and it had been the

panther. It was Mrs Habersham who was holding back the quilt for the others to go in and look at the bed where Drusilla slept and then showing them the pallet where Father and I slept. Then she saw me and said, 'And who is this?'

'That's Bayard,' Mrs Compson said.

'You poor child,' Mrs Habersham said. So I didn't stop. But I couldn't help but hear them. It sounded like a ladies' club meeting with Mrs Habersham running it, because every now and then Mrs Habersham would forget to whisper: ' – Mother should come, be sent for at once. But lacking her presence ... we, the ladies of the community, mothers ourselves ... child probably taken advantage of by gallant romantic ... before realizing the price she must – ' and Mrs Compson said, 'Hush! Hush!' and then somebody else said, 'Do you really suppose –' and then Mrs Habersham forgot to whisper good: 'What else? What other reason can you name why she should choose to conceal herself down there in the woods all day long, lifting heavy weights like logs and – '

Then I went away. I filled the bucket at the spring and went back to the log-yard where Drusilla and Ringo and Joby were feeding the bandsaw and the blindfolded mule going round and round in the sawdust. And then Joby kind of made a sound and we all stopped and looked and there was Mrs Habersham, with three of the others kind of peeping out from behind her with their eyes round and bright, looking at Drusilla standing there in the sawdust and shavings, in her dirty sweated overalls and shirt and brogans, with her face sweat-streaked with sawdust and her short hair yellow with it. 'I am Martha Habersham,' Mrs Habersham said. 'I am a neighbour and I hope to be a friend.' And then she said, 'You poor child.'

We just looked at her; when Drusilla finally spoke, she sounded like Ringo and I would when Father would say something to us in Latin for a joke. 'Ma'am?' Drusilla said. Because I was just fifteen; I still didn't know what it was all about; I just stood there and listened without even thinking much, like when they had been talking in the cabin. 'My condition?' Drusilla said. 'My – '

'Yes,' Mrs Habersham said. 'No mother, no woman to ... forced to these straits – ' kind of waving her hand at the mules that hadn't stopped and at Joby and Ringo goggling at her and the three others still peeping around her at Drusilla, ' – to offer you not only our help, but our sympathy.'

'My condition,' Drusilla said. 'My con . . . Help and sym –' Then she began to say, 'Oh. Oh. Oh,' standing there, and then she was running. She began to run like a deer, that starts to run and then decides where it wants to go; she turned right in the air and came towards me, running light over the logs and planks, with her mouth open, saying 'John, John' not loud; for a minute it was like she thought I was Father until she waked up and found I was not; she stopped without even ceasing to run, like a bird stops in the air, motionless yet still furious with movement. 'Is that what you think too?' she said. Then she was gone. Every now and then I could see her footprints, spaced and fast, just inside the woods, but when I came out of the bottom, I couldn't see her. But the surreys and buggies were still in front of the cabin and I could see Mrs Compson and the other ladies on the porch, looking out across the pasture towards the bottom, so I did not go there. But before I came to the other cabin, where Louvinia and Joby and Ringo lived, I saw Louvinia come up the hill from the spring, carrying her cedar water bucket and singing. Then she went into the cabin and the singing stopped short off and so I knew where Drusilla was. But I didn't hide. I went to the window and looked in and saw Drusilla just turning from where she had been leaning her head in her arms on the mantel when Louvinia came in with the water bucket and a gum twig in her mouth and Father's old hat on top of her head rag. Drusilla was crying. 'That's what it is, then,' she said. 'Coming down there to the mill and telling me that in my condition – sympathy and help – Strangers; I never saw any of them before and I don't care a damn what they – But you and Bayard. Is that what you believe? that John and I – that we –' Then Louvinia moved. Her hand came out quicker than Drusilla could jerk back and lay flat on the belly of Drusilla's overalls, then Louvinia was holding Drusilla in her arms like she used to hold me and Drusilla was crying hard. 'That John and I – that we – And Gavin dead at Shiloh and John's home burned and his plantation ruined, that he and I – We went to the war to hurt Yankees, not hunting women!'

'I knows you ain't,' Louvinia said. 'Hush now. Hush.'

And that's about all. It didn't take them long. I don't know whether Mrs Habersham made Mrs Compson send for Aunt Louisa or whether Aunt Louisa just gave them a deadline and then came herself. Because we were busy, Drusilla and Joby and Ringo and me at the mill, and Father in town; we wouldn't see him from the time he would ride away in the morning until when he would get back, sometimes late, at night. Because they were strange times then. For four years we had lived for just one thing, even the women and children who could not fight: to get Yankee troops out of the country; we thought that when that happened, it would be all over. And now that had happened, and then before the summer began I heard Father say to Drusilla, 'We were promised Federal troops; Lincoln himself promised to send us troops. Then things will be all right.' That, from a man who had commanded a regiment for four years with the avowed purpose of driving Federal troops from the country. Now it was as though we had not surrendered at all, we had joined forces with the men who had been our enemies against a new foe whose means we could not always fathom but whose aim we could always dread. So he was busy in town all day long. They were building Jefferson back, the courthouse and the stores, but it was more than that which Father and the other men were doing; it was something which he would not let Drusilla or me or Ringo go into town to see. Then one day Ringo slipped off and went to town and came back and he looked at me with his eyes rolling a little.

'Do you know what I ain't?' he said.

'What?' I said.

'I ain't a nigger any more. I done been abolished.' Then I asked him what he was, if he wasn't a nigger any more and he showed me what he had in his hand. It was a new scrip dollar; it was drawn on the United States Resident Treasurer, Yoknapatawpha County, Mississippi, and signed, 'Cassius Q. Benbow, Acting Marshal' in a neat clerk's hand, with a big sprawling X under it.

'Cassius Q. Benbow?' I said.

'Co-rect,' Ringo said. 'Uncle Cash that druv the Benbow carriage twell he run off with the Yankees two years ago. He back now and he gonter be elected Marshal of Jefferson. That's what Marse John and the other white folks is so busy about.'

'A nigger?' I said. 'A nigger?'

'No,' Ringo said. 'They ain't no more niggers in Jefferson nor nowhere else.' Then he told me about the two Burdens from Missouri, with a patent from Washington to organize the niggers into Republicans, and how Father and the other men were trying to prevent it. 'Naw, suh,' he said. 'This war ain't over. Hit just started good. Used to be when you seed a Yankee you knowed him because he never had nothing but a gun or a mule halter or a handful of hen feathers. Now you don't even know him and stid of the gun he got a clutch of this stuff in one hand and a clutch of nigger voting tickets in the yuther.' So we were busy; we just saw Father at night and sometimes then Ringo and I and even Drusilla would take one look at him and we wouldn't ask him any questions. So it didn't take them long, because Drusilla was already beaten; she was just marking time without knowing it from that afternoon when the fourteen ladies got into the surreys and buggies and went back to town until one afternoon about two months later when we heard Denny hollering even before the wagon came in the gates, and Aunt Louisa sitting on one of the trunks (that's what beat Drusilla: the trunks. They had her dresses in them that she hadn't worn in three years; Ringo never had seen her in a dress until Aunt Louisa came) in mourning, even to the crêpe bow on her umbrella handle, that hadn't worn mourning when we were at Hawkhurst two years ago though Uncle Dennison was just as dead then as he was now. She came to the cabin and got out of the wagon, already crying and talking just like the letters sounded, like even when you listened to her you had to skip round fast to make any sense:

'I have come to appeal to them once more with a mother's tears though I don't think it will do any good though I had prayed until the very last that this boy's innocence might be spared and preserved but what must be must be and at least we can all three bear our burden together'; sitting in Granny's chair in the middle of the room, without even laying down the umbrella or taking her bonnet off, looking at the pallet where Father and I slept and then at the quilt nailed to the rafter to make a room for Drusilla, dabbing at her mouth with a handkerchief that made the whole cabin smell like dead roses. And then Drusilla came in from the mill, in the muddy brogans and the sweaty shirt and overalls and her hair sunburned and full of sawdust, and Aunt Louisa looked at her once and begun to cry again, saying, 'Lost, lost. Thank God in His mercy that Dennison Hawk was taken before he lived to see what I see.'

She was already beaten. Aunt Louisa made her put on a dress that night; we watched her run out of the cabin in it and run down the hill towards the spring while we were waiting for Father. And he came and walked into the cabin where Aunt Louisa was still sitting in Granny's chair with the handkerchief before her mouth. 'This is a pleasant surprise, Miss Louisa,' Father said.

'It is not pleasant to me, Colonel Sartoris,' Aunt Louisa said. 'And after a year, I suppose I cannot call it surprise. But it is still a shock.' So Father came out too and we went down to the spring and found Drusilla hiding behind the big beech, crouched down like she was trying to hide the skirt from Father even while he raised her up. 'What's a dress?' he said. 'It don't matter. Come. Get up, soldier.'

But she was beaten, like as soon as she let them put the dress on her she was whipped; like in the dress she could neither fight back nor run away. And so she didn't come down to the logyard any more, and now that Father and I slept in the cabin with Joby and Ringo, I didn't even see Drusilla except at mealtime. And we were busy getting the timber out, and now everybody was talking about the election and how Father had told the two Burdens before all the men in town that the election would never be held with Cash Benbow or any other nigger in it and how the Burdens had dared him to stop it. And besides, the other cabin would be full of Jefferson ladies all day; you would have thought that Drusilla was Mrs Habersham's daughter and not Aunt Louisa's. They would begin to arrive right after breakfast and stay all day, so that at supper Aunt Louisa would sit in her black mourning except for the bonnet and umbrella, with a wad of some kind of black knitting she carried round with her and that never got finished and the folded handkerchief handy in her belt (only she ate fine; she ate more than

Father even because the election was just a week off and I reckon he was thinking about the Burdens) and refusing to speak to anybody except Denny; and Drusilla trying to eat, with her face strained and thin and her eyes like somebody's that had been whipped a long time now and is going just on nerve.

Then Drusilla broke; they beat her. Because she was strong; she wasn't much older than I was, but she had let Aunt Louisa and Mrs Habersham choose the game and she had beat them both until that night when Aunt Louisa went behind her back and chose a game she couldn't beat. I was coming up to supper; I heard them inside the cabin before I could stop: 'Can't you believe me?' Drusilla said. 'Can't you understand that in the troop I was just another man and not much of one at that, and since we came home here I am just another mouth for John to feed, just a cousin of John's wife and not much older than his own son?' And I could almost see Aunt Louisa sitting there with that knitting that never progressed:

'You wish to tell me that you, a young woman, associated with him, a still young man, day and night for a year, running about the country with no guard nor check of any sort upon – Do you take me for a complete fool?' So that night Aunt Louisa beat her; we had just sat down to supper when Aunt Louisa looked at me like she had been waiting for the noise of the bench to stop: 'Bayard, I do not ask your forgiveness for this because it is your burden too; you are an innocent victim as well as Dennison and I –' Then she looked at Father, thrust back in Granny's chair (the only chair we had) in her black dress, the black wad of knitting beside her plate. 'Colonel Sartoris,' she said, 'I am a woman; I must request what the husband whom I have lost and the man son which I have not would demand, perhaps at the point of a pistol – Will you marry my daughter?'

I got out. I moved fast; I heard the light sharp sound when Drusilla's head went down between her flung-out arms on the table, and the sound the bench made when Father got up too; I passed him standing beside Drusilla with his hand on her head. 'They have beat you, Drusilla,' he said.

3

Mrs Habersham got there before we had finished breakfast the next morning. I don't know how Aunt Louisa got word in to her so quick. But there she was, and she and Aunt Louisa set the wedding for the day after tomorrow. I don't reckon they even knew that that was the day Father had told the Burdens Cash Benbow would never be elected marshal in Jefferson. I don't reckon they paid any more attention to it than if all the men had decided that day after tomorrow all the clocks in Jefferson were to be set back or up an hour. Maybe they didn't even know there was to be an election, that all the men in the county would be riding towards Jefferson tomorrow with pistols in their pockets, and that the Burdens already had their nigger voters camped in a cotton gin on the edge of town under guard. I don't reckon they even cared. Because like Father said, women cannot believe that anything can be right or wrong or even be very important that can be decided by a lot of little scraps of scribbled paper dropped into a box.

It was to be a big wedding; all Jefferson was to be invited and Mrs Habersham planning to bring the three bottles of Madeira she had been saving for five years now when Aunt Louisa began to cry again. But they caught on quick now; now all of them were patting Aunt Louisa's hands and giving her vinegar to smell and Mrs Habersham saying, 'Of course. You poor thing. A public wedding now, after a year, would be a public notice of the . . .' So they decided it would be a reception, because Mrs Habersham said how a reception could be held for a bridal couple at any time, even ten years later. So Drusilla was to ride into town, meet Father and be married as quick and quiet as possible, with just me and one other for witnesses to make it legal; none of the ladies themselves would even be present. Then they would come back home and we would have the reception.

So they began to arrive early the next morning, with baskets of food and tablecloths and silver like for a church supper. Mrs Habersham brought a veil and a wreath and they all helped Drusilla to dress, only Aunt Louisa made Drusilla put on

Father's big riding cloak over the veil and wreath too, and
Ringo brought the horses up, all curried and brushed, and I
helped Drusilla on with Aunt Louisa and the others all watching from the porch. But I didn't know that Ringo was missing
when we started, not even when I heard Aunt Louisa hollering
for Denny while we rode down the drive. It was Louvinia that
told about it, about how after we left the ladies set and decorated the table and spread the wedding breakfast and how they
were all watching the gate and Aunt Louisa still hollering for
Denny now and then when they saw Ringo and Denny come
up the drive riding double on one of the mules at a gallop, with
Denny's eyes round as doorknobs and already hollering. 'They
kilt um! They kilt um!'

'Who?' Aunt Louisa hollered. 'Where have you been?'

'To town!' Denny hollered. 'Them two Burdens! They
kilt um!'

'Who killed them?' Aunt Louisa hollered.

'Drusilla and Cousin John!' Denny hollered. Then Louvinia said how Aunt Louisa hollered sure enough.

'Do you mean to tell me that Drusilla and that man are not
married yet?'

Because we didn't have time. Maybe Drusilla and Father
would have, but when we came into the square we saw the
crowd of niggers kind of huddled beyond the hotel door with
six or eight strange white men herding them, and then all of a
sudden I saw the Jefferson men, the men that I knew, that
Father knew, running across the square towards the hotel with
each one holding his hip like a man runs with a pistol in his
pocket. And then I saw the men who were Father's troop lined
up before the hotel door, blocking it off. And then I was sliding
off my horse too and watching Drusilla struggling with George
Wyatt. But he didn't have hold of her, he just had hold of the
cloak, and then she was through the line of them and running
towards the hotel with her wreath on one side of her head and
the veil streaming behind. But George held me. He threw the
cloak down and held me. 'Let go,' I said. 'Father.'

'Steady, now,' George said, holding me. 'John's just gone in
to vote.'

'But there are two of them!' I said. 'Let me go!'

'John's got two shots in the derringer,' George said. 'Steady, now.'

But they held me. And then we heard the three shots and we all turned and looked at the door. I don't know how long it was. 'The last two was that derringer,' George said. I don't know how long it was. The old nigger that was Mrs Holston's porter, that was too old even to be free, stuck his head out once and said 'Gret Gawd' and ducked back. Then Drusilla came out, carrying the ballot box, the wreath on one side of her head and the veil twisted about her arm, and then Father came out behind her, brushing his new beaver hat on his sleeve. And then it was loud; I could hear them when they drew in their breath like when the Yankees used to hear it begin:

'Yaaaaa – ' But Father raised his hand and they stopped. Then you couldn't hear anything.

'We heard a pistol too,' George said. 'Did they touch you?'

'No,' Father said. 'I let them fire first. You all heard. You boys can swear to my derringer.'

'Yes,' George said. 'We all heard.' Now Father looked at all of them, at all the faces in sight, slow.

'Does any man here want a word with me about this?' he said. But you could not hear anything, not even moving. The herd of niggers stood like they had when I first saw them, with the Northern white men herding them together. Father put his hat on and took the ballot box from Drusilla and helped her back on to her horse and handed the ballot box up to her. Then he looked around again, at all of them. 'This election will be held out at my home,' he said. 'I hereby appoint Drusilla Hawk voting commissioner until the votes are cast and counted. Does any man here object?' But he stopped them again with his hand before it had begun good. 'Not now, boys,' he said. He turned to Drusilla. 'Go home, I will go to the sheriff, and then I will follow you.'

'Like hell you will,' George Wyatt said. 'Some of the boys will ride out with Drusilla. The rest of us will come with you.'

But Father would not let them. 'Don't you see we are working for peace through law and order?' he said. 'I will make bond and then follow you. You do as I say.' So we went on; we turned in the gates with Drusilla in front, the ballot box on her pommel – us and Father's men and about a hundred more, and rode on up to the cabin where the buggies and surreys were standing, and Drusilla passed the ballot box to me and got down and took the box again and was walking towards the cabin when she stopped dead still. I reckon she and I both remembered at the same time and I reckon that even the others, the men, knew all of a sudden that something was wrong. Because like Father said, I reckon women don't ever surrender: not only victory, but not even defeat. Because that's how we were stopped when Aunt Louisa and the other ladies came out on the porch, and then Father shoved past me and jumped down beside Drusilla. But Aunt Louisa never even looked at him.

'So you are not married,' she said.

'I forgot,' Drusilla said.

'You forgot? You *forgot?*'

'I . . . ' Drusilla said. 'We . . .'

Now Aunt Louisa looked at us; she looked along the line of us sitting there in our saddles; she looked at me too just like she did at the others, like she had never seen me before. 'And who are these, pray? Your wedding train of forgetters? Your groomsmen of murder and robbery?'

'They came to vote,' Drusilla said.

'To vote,' Aunt Louisa said. 'Ah. To vote. Since you have forced your mother and brother to live under a roof of licence and adultery you think you can also force them to live in a polling booth refuge from violence and bloodshed, do you? Bring me that box.' But Drusilla didn't move, standing there in her torn dress and the ruined veil and the twisted wreath hanging from her hair by a few pins. Aunt Louisa came down the steps; we didn't know what she was going to do: we just sat there and watched her snatch the polling box from Drusilla and fling it across the yard. 'Come into the house,' she said.

'No,' Drusilla said.

'Come into the house. I will send for a minister myself.'

'No,' Drusilla said. 'This is an election. Don't you understand? I am voting commissioner.'

'So you refuse?'

'I have to. I must.' She sounded like a little girl that has been caught playing in the mud. 'John said that I – '

Then Aunt Louisa began to cry. She stood there in the black dress, without the knitting and for the first time that I ever saw it, without even the handkerchief, crying, until Mrs Habersham came and led her back into the house. Then they voted. That didn't take long either. They set the box on the sawchunk where Louvinia washed, and Ringo got the pokeberry juice and an old piece of window shade, and they cut it into ballots. 'Let all who want the Honourable Cassius Q. Benbow to be Marshal of Jefferson write Yes on his ballot; opposed, No,' Father said.

'And I'll do the writing and save some more time,' George Wyatt said. So he made a pack of the ballots and wrote them against his saddle and fast as he would write them the men would take them and drop them into the box and Drusilla would call their names out. We could hear Aunt Louisa still crying inside the cabin and we could see the other ladies watching us through the window. It didn't take long. 'You needn't bother to count them,' George said. 'They all voted No.'

And that's all. They rode back to town then, carrying the box, with Father and Drusilla in the torn wedding dress and the crooked wreath and veil standing beside the sawchunk, watching them. Only this time even Father could not have stopped them. It came back high and thin and ragged and fierce, like when the Yankees used to hear it out of the smoke and the galloping:

'Yaaaaay, Drusilla!' they hollered. 'Yaaaaaay, John Sartoris! Yaaaaaaay!'

An Odour of Verbena

I

It was just after supper. I had just opened my *Coke* on the table beneath the lamp; I heard Professor Wilkins' feet in the hall and then the instant of silence as he put his hand to the doorknob, and I should have known. People talk glibly of presentiment, but I had none. I heard his feet on the stairs and then in the hall approaching and there was nothing in the feet because although I had lived in his house for three college years now and although both he and Mrs Wilkins called me Bayard in the house, he would no more have entered my room without knocking than I would have entered his – or hers. Then he flung the door violently inward against the doorstop with one of those gestures with or by which an almost painfully unflagging preceptory of youth ultimately aberrates, and stood there saying, 'Bayard, Bayard, my son, my dear son.'

I should have known; I should have been prepared. Or maybe I was prepared because I remember how I closed the book carefully, even marking the place, before I rose. He (Professor Wilkins) was doing something, bustling at something; it was my hat and cloak which he handed me and which I took although I would not need the cloak, unless even then I was thinking (although it was October, the equinox had not occurred) that the rains and the cool weather would arrive before I should see this room again and so I would need the cloak anyway to return to it if I returned, thinking 'God, if he had only done this last night, flung that door crashing and bouncing against the stop last night without knocking so I could have gotten there before it happened, been there when it did, beside him on whatever spot, wherever it was that he would have to fall and lie in the dust and dirt.'

'Your boy is downstairs in the kitchen,' he said. It was not until years later that he told me (someone did; it must have been Judge Wilkins) how Ringo had apparently flung the cook aside and come on into the house and into the library where he and Mrs Wilkins were sitting and said without preamble and already turning to withdraw: 'They shot Colonel Sartoris this morning. Tell him I be waiting in the kitchen' and was gone before either of them could move. 'He has ridden forty miles yet he refuses to eat anything.' We were moving towards the door now – the door on my side of which I had lived for three years now with what I knew, what I knew now I must have believed and expected, yet beyond which I had heard the approaching feet yet heard nothing in the feet. 'If there was just anything I could do.'

'Yes, sir,' I said. 'A fresh horse for my boy. He will want to go back with me.'

'By all means take mine – Mrs Wilkins',' he cried. His tone was no different yet he did cry it and I suppose that at the same moment we both realized that was funny – a short-legged deep-barrelled mare who looked exactly like a spinster music teacher, which Mrs Wilkins drove to a basket phaeton – which was good for me, like being doused with a pail of cold water would have been good for me.

'Thank you, sir,' I said. 'We won't need it. I will get a fresh horse for him at the livery stable when I get my mare.' Good for me, because even before I finished speaking I knew that would not be necessary either, that Ringo would have stopped at the livery stable before he came out to the college and attended to that and that the fresh horse for him and my mare both would be saddled and waiting now at the side fence and we would not have to go through Oxford at all. Loosh would not have thought of that if he had come for me, he would have come straight to the college, to Professor Wilkins', and told his news, and then sat down and let me take charge from then on. But not Ringo.

He followed me from the room. From now until Ringo and I rode away into the hot thick dusty darkness quick and strained for the overdue equinox like a labouring delayed woman, he would be somewhere either just beside me or just behind me and I never to know exactly nor care which. He was trying to find the words with which to offer me his pistol too. I could almost hear him: 'Ah, this unhappy land, not ten years recovered from the fever yet still men must kill one another, still we must pay Cain's price in his own coin.' But he did not actually

say it. He just followed me, somewhere beside or behind me as
we descended the stairs towards where Mrs Wilkins waited in
the hall beneath the chandelier – a thin, grey woman who
reminded me of Granny, not that she looked like Granny probably but because she had known Granny – a lifted anxious still
face which was thinking *Who lives by the sword shall die by it* just
as Granny would have thought, towards which I walked, had
to walk not because I was Granny's grandson and had lived in
her house for three college years and was about the age of her
son when he was killed in almost the last battle nine years ago,
but because I was now The Sartoris. (The Sartoris: that had
been one of the concomitant flashes, along with the *at last it has
happened* when Professor Wilkins opened my door.) She didn't
offer me a horse and pistol, not because she liked me any less
than Professor Wilkins, but because she was a woman and so
wiser than any man, else the men would not have gone on with
the War for two years after they knew they were whipped. She
just put her hands (a small woman, no bigger than Granny had
been) on my shoulders and said, 'Give my love to Drusilla and
your Aunt Jenny. And come back when you can.'

'Only I don't know when that will be,' I said. 'I don't know
how many things I will have to attend to.' Yes, I lied even to
her; it had not been but a minute yet since he had flung that
door bouncing into the stop yet already I was beginning to
realize, to become aware of that which I still had no yardstick
to measure save that one consisting of what, despite myself,
despite my raising and background (or maybe because of them)
I had for some time known I was becoming and had feared the
test of it; I remember how I thought while her hands still rested
on my shoulders: *At least this will be my chance to find out if I am
what I think I am or if I just hope; if I am going to do what I have taught
myself is right or if I am just going to wish I were.*

We went on to the kitchen, Professor Wilkins still somewhere beside or behind me and still offering me the pistol and
horse in a dozen different ways. Ringo was waiting; I remember
how I thought then that no matter what might happen to either
of us, I would never be The Sartoris to him. He was twenty-
four too, but in a way he had changed even less than I had since
that day when we had nailed Grumby's body to the door of the

old compress. Maybe it was because he had outgrown me, had changed so much that summer while he and Granny traded mules with the Yankees that since then I had had to do most of the changing just to catch up with him. He was sitting quietly in a chair beside the cold stove, spent-looking too who had ridden forty miles (at one time, either in Jefferson or when he was alone at last on the road somewhere, he had cried; dust was now caked and dried in the tear-channels on his face) and would ride forty more yet would not eat, looking up at me a little red-eyed with weariness (or maybe it was more than just weariness and so I would never catch up with him) then rising without a word and going on towards the door and I following and Professor Wilkins still offering the horse and the pistol without speaking the words and still thinking (I could feel that too) *Dies by the sword. Dies by the sword.*

Ringo had the two horses saddled at the side gate, as I had known he would – the fresh one for himself and my mare father had given me three years ago, that could do a mile under two minutes any day and a mile every eight minutes all day long. He was already mounted when I realized that what Professor Wilkins wanted was to shake my hand. We shook hands; I knew he believed he was touching flesh which might not be alive tomorrow night and I thought for a second how if I told him what I was going to do, since we had talked about it, about how if there was anything at all in the Book, anything of hope and peace for His blind and bewildered spawn which He had chosen above all others to offer immortality, *Thou shalt not kill* must be it, since maybe he even believed that he had taught it to me except that he had not, nobody had, not even myself since it went further than just having been learned. But I did not tell him. He was too old to be forced so, to condone even in principle such a decision; he was too old to have to stick to principle in the face of blood and raising and background, to be faced without warning and made to deliver like by a highwayman out of the dark: only the young could do that – one still young enough to have his youth supplied him gratis as a reason (not an excuse) for cowardice.

So I said nothing. I just shook his hand and mounted too, and Ringo and I rode on. We would not have to pass through

Oxford now and so soon (there was a thin sickle of moon like the heel print of a boot in wet sand) the road to Jefferson lay before us, the road which I had travelled for the first time three years ago with Father and travelled twice at Christmas time and then in June and September and twice at Christmas time again and then June and September again each college term since alone on the mare, not even knowing that this was peace; and now this time and maybe last time who would not die (I knew that) but who maybe forever after could never again hold up his head. The horses took the gait which they would hold for forty miles. My mare knew the long road ahead and Ringo had a good beast too, had talked Hilliard at the livery stable out of a good horse too. Maybe it was the tears, the channels of dried mud across which his strain-reddened eyes had looked at me, but I rather think it was that same quality which used to enable him to replenish his and Granny's supply of United States Army letterheads during that time – some outrageous assurance gained from too long and too close association with white people: the one whom he called Granny, the other with whom he had slept from the time we were born until Father rebuilt the house. We spoke one time, then no more:

'We could bushwhack him,' he said. 'Like we done Grumby that day. But I reckon that wouldn't suit that white skin you walks around in.'

'No,' I said. We rode on; it was October; there was plenty of time still for verbena although I would have to reach home before I would realize there was a need for it; plenty of time for verbena yet from the garden where Aunt Jenny puttered beside old Joby, in a pair of Father's old cavalry gauntlets, among the coaxed and ordered beds, the quaint and odorous old names, for though it was October no rain had come yet and hence no frost to bring (or leave behind) the first half-warm half-chill nights of Indian Summer – the drowsing air cool and empty for geese yet languid still with the old hot dusty smell of fox grape and sassafras – the nights when before I became a man and went to college to learn law Ringo and I, with lantern and axe and crokersack and six dogs (one to follow the trail and five more just for the tonguing, the music) would hunt possum in the pasture where, hidden, we had seen our first Yankee that afternoon on the bright horse, where for the last year now you could hear the whistling of the trains which had no longer belonged to Mr Redmond for a long while now and which at some instant, some second during the morning Father too had relinquished along with the pipe which Ringo said he was smoking, which slipped from his hand as he fell. We rode on, towards the house where he would be lying in the parlour now, in his regimentals (sabre too) and where Drusilla would be waiting for me beneath all the festive glitter of the chandeliers, in the yellow ball gown and the sprig of verbena in her hair, holding the two loaded pistols (I could see that too, who had had no presentiment; I could see her, in the formal brilliant room arranged formally for obsequy, not tall, not slender as a woman is but as a youth, a boy, is motionless, in yellow, the face calm, almost bemused, the head simple and severe, the balancing sprig of verbena above each ear, the two arms bent at the elbows, the two hands shoulder high, the two identical duelling pistols lying upon, not clutched in, one to each: the Greek amphora priestess of a succinct and formal violence).

2

Drusilla said that he had a dream. I was twenty then and she and I would walk in the garden in the summer twilight while we waited for Father to ride in from the railroad. I was just twenty then: that summer before I entered the University to take the law degree which Father decided I should have and four years after the one, the day, the evening when Father and Drusilla had kept old Cash Benbow from becoming United States Marshal and returned home still unmarried and Mrs Habersham herded them into her carriage and drove them back to town and dug her husband out of his little dim hole in the new bank and made him sign Father's peace bond for killing the two carpet baggers, and took Father and Drusilla to the minister herself and saw that they were married. And Father had rebuilt the house too, on the same blackened spot, over the same cellar, where the other had burned, only larger, much larger: Drusilla said that the house was the aura of Father's dream just as a bride's trousseau and veil is the aura of hers. And Aunt Jenny had come to live with us now so we had the garden (Drusilla would no more have bothered with flowers than Father himself would have, who even now, even four years after it was over, still seemed to exist, breathe, in that last year of it while she had ridden in man's clothes and with her hair cut short like any other member of Father's troop, across Georgia and both Carolinas in front of Sherman's army) for her to gather sprigs of verbena from to wear in her hair because she said verbena was the only scent you could smell above the smell of horses and courage, and so it was the only one that was worth the wearing. The railroad was hardly begun then and Father and Mr Redmond were not only still partners, they were still friends, which as George Wyatt said was easily a record for Father, and he would leave the house at daybreak on Jupiter, riding up and down the unfinished line with two saddlebags of gold coins borrowed on Friday to pay the men on Saturday, keeping just two cross-ties ahead of the sheriff as Aunt Jenny said. So we walked in the dusk, slowly between Aunt Jenny's flower beds while Drusilla (in a dress now, who still would have worn pants all the time if Father had let her) leaned lightly on my arm and I smelled the verbena in her hair as I had smelled the rain in it and in Father's beard that night four years ago when he and Drusilla and Uncle Buck McCaslin found Grumby and then came home and found Ringo and me more than just asleep; escaped into that oblivion which God or Nature or whoever it was had supplied us with for the time being, who had had to perform more than should be required of children because there should be some limit to the age, the youth at least below which one should not have to kill. This was just after the Saturday night when he returned and I watched him clean the derringer and reload it and we learned that the dead man was almost a neighbour, a hill man who had been in the first infantry regiment when it voted Father out of command: and we never to know if the man actually intended to rob Father or not because Father had shot too quick, but only that he had a wife and several children in a dirt-floored cabin in the hills, to whom Father the next day sent some money and she (the wife) walked into the house two days later while we were sitting at the dinner-table and flung the money at Father's face.

'But nobody could have more of a dream than Colonel Sutpen,' I said. He had been Father's second-in-command in the first regiment and had been elected colonel when the regiment deposed Father after Second Manassas, and it was Sutpen and not the regiment whom father never forgave. He was underbred, a cold ruthless man who had come into the country about thirty years before the War, nobody knew from where except Father said you could look at him and know he would not dare to tell. He had got some land and nobody knew how he did that either, and he got money from somewhere – Father said they all believed he robbed steam-boats, either as a card sharper or as an out-and-out highwayman – and built a big house and married and set up as a gentleman. Then he lost everything in the War like everybody else, all hope of descendants too (his son killed his daughter's fiancé on the eve of the wedding and vanished) yet he came back home and set out single-handed to rebuild his plantation. He had no friends to borrow from and he had nobody to leave it to and he was past sixty years old, yet he set out to rebuild his place like it used to be; they told how he was too busy to bother with politics or anything; how when Father and the other men organized the nightriders to keep the carpet baggers from organizing the Negroes into an insurrection, he refused to have anything to do with it. Father stopped hating him long enough to ride out to see Sutpen himself and he (Sutpen) came to the door with a lamp and did not even invite them to come in and discuss it; Father said, 'Are you with us or against us?' and he said, 'I'm for my land. If every man of you would rehabilitate his own land, the country will take care of itself' and Father challenged him to bring the lamp out and set it on a stump where they could both see to shoot and Sutpen would not. 'Nobody could have more of a dream than that.'

'Yes. But his dream is just Sutpen. John's is not. He is thinking of this whole country which he is trying to raise by its bootstraps, so that all the people in it, not just his kind nor his old regiment, but all the people, black and white, the women and children back in the hills who don't even own shoes – Don't you see?'

'But how can they get any good from what he wants to do for them if they are – after he has –'

'Killed some of them? I suppose you include those two carpet baggers he had to kill to hold that first election, don't you?'

'They were men. Human beings.'

'They were Northerners, foreigners who had no business here. They were pirates.' We walked on, her weight hardly discernible on my arm, her head just reaching my shoulder. I had always been a little taller than she, even on that night at Hawkhurst while we listened to the niggers passing in the road, and she had changed but little since – the same boy-hard body, the close implacable head with its savagely cropped hair which I had watched from the wagon above the tide of crazed singing niggers as we went down into the river – the body not slender as women are but as boys are slender. 'A dream is not a very safe thing to be near, Bayard. I know; I had one once. It's like a loaded pistol with a hair trigger: if it stays alive long enough, somebody is going to be hurt. But if it's a good dream, it's worth it. There are not many dreams in the world, but there are a lot of human lives. And one human life or two dozen – '

'Are not worth anything?'

'No. Not anything – Listen. I hear Jupiter. I'll beat you to the house.' She was already running, the skirts she did not like to wear lifted almost to her knees, her legs beneath it running as boys run just as she rode like men ride.

I was twenty then. But the next time I was twenty-four; I had been three years at the University and in another two weeks I would ride back to Oxford for the final year and my degree. It was just last summer, last August, and Father had just beat Redmond for the State legislature. The railroad was finished now and the partnership between Father and Redmond had been dissolved so long ago that most people would have forgotten they were ever partners if it hadn't been for the enmity between them. There had been a third partner but nobody hardly remembered his name now; he and his name both had vanished in the fury of the conflict which set up between Father and Redmond almost before they began to lay the rails, between Father's violent and ruthless dictatorialness and will to dominate (the idea was his; he did think of the railroad first and then took Redmond in) and that quality in Redmond (as George

Wyatt said, he was not a coward or Father would never have teamed with him) which permitted him to stand as much as he did from Father, to bear and bear and bear until something (not his will nor his courage) broke in him. During the War Redmond had not been a soldier, he had had something to do with cotton for the Government; he could have made money himself out of it but he had not and everybody knew he had not, Father knew it, yet Father would even taunt him with not having smelled powder. He was wrong; he knew he was when it was too late for him to stop just as a drunkard reaches a point where it is too late for him to stop, where he promises himself that he will and maybe believes he will or can but it is too late. Finally they reached the point (they had both put everything they could mortgage or borrow into it for Father to ride up and down the line, paying the workmen and the waybills on the rails at the last possible instant) where even Father realized that one of them would have to get out. So (they were not speaking then; it was arranged by Judge Benbow) they met and agreed to buy or sell, naming a price which, in reference to what they had put into it, was ridiculously low but which each believed the other could not raise – at least Father claimed that Redmond did not believe he could raise it. So Redmond accepted the price, and found out that Father had the money. And according to Father, that's what started it, although Uncle Buck McCaslin said Father could not have owned a half interest in even one hog, let alone a railroad, and not dissolve the business either sworn enemy or death-pledged friend to his recent partner. So they parted and Father finished the road. By that time, seeing that he was going to finish it, some Northern people sold him a locomotive on credit which he named for Aunt Jenny, with a silver oil can in the cab with her name engraved on it; and last summer the first train ran into Jefferson, the engine decorated with flowers and Father in the cab blowing blast after blast on the whistle when he passed Redmond's house; and there were speeches at the station, with more flowers and a Confederate flag and girls in white dresses and red sashes and a band, and Father stood on the pilot of the engine and made a direct and absolutely needless allusion to Mr Redmond. That was it. He wouldn't let him alone. George

Wyatt came to me right afterwards and told me. 'Right or wrong,' he said, 'us boys and most of the other folks in this county know John's right. But he ought to let Redmond alone. I know what's wrong: he's had to kill too many folks, and that's bad for a man. We all know Colonel's brave as a lion, but Redmond ain't no coward either and there ain't any use in making a brave man that made one mistake eat crow all the time. Can't you talk to him?'

'I don't know,' I said. 'I'll try.' But I had no chance. That is, I could have talked to him and he would have listened, but he could not have heard me because he had stepped straight from the pilot of that engine into the race for the Legislature. Maybe he knew that Redmond would have to oppose him to save his face even though he (Redmond) must have known that, after that train ran into Jefferson, he had no chance against Father, or maybe Redmond had already announced his candidacy and Father entered the race just because of that, I don't remember. Anyway they ran, a bitter contest in which Father continued to badger Redmond without reason or need, since they both knew it would be a landslide for Father. And it was, and we thought he was satisfied. Maybe he thought so himself, as the drunkard believes that he is done with drink; and it was that afternoon and Drusilla and I walked in the garden in the twilight and I said something about what George Wyatt had told me and she released my arm and turned me to face her and said, 'This from you? You? Have you forgotten Grumby?'

'No,' I said. 'I never will forget him.'

'You never will. I wouldn't let you. There are worse things than killing men, Bayard. There are worse things than being killed. Sometimes I think the finest thing that can happen to a man is to love something, a woman preferably, well, hard hard hard, then to die young because he believed what he could not help but believe and was what he could not (could not? would not) help but be.' Now she was looking at me in a way she never had before. I did not know what it meant then and was not to know until tonight since neither of us knew then that two months later Father would be dead. I just knew that she was looking at me as she never had before and that the scent of the verbena in her hair seemed to have increased a hundred times, to have got a hundred times stronger, to be everywhere in the dusk in which something was about to happen which I had never dreamed of. Then she spoke. 'Kiss me, Bayard.'

'No. You are Father's wife.'

'And eight years older than you are. And your fourth cousin too. And I have black hair. Kiss me, Bayard.'

'No.'

'Kiss me, Bayard.' So I leaned my face down to her. But she didn't move, standing so, bent lightly back from me from the waist, looking at me; now it was she who said, 'No.' So I put my arms around her. Then she came to me, melted as women will and can, the arms with the wrist- and elbow-power to control horses about my shoulders, using the wrists to hold my face to hers until there was no longer need for the wrists; I thought then of the woman of thirty, the symbol of the ancient and eternal Snake and of the men who have written of her, and I realized then the immitigable chasm between all life and all print – that those who can, do, those who cannot and suffer enough because they can't, write about it. Then I was free, I could see her again, I saw her still watching me with that dark inscrutable look, looking up at me now across her down-slanted face; I watched her arms rise with almost the exact gesture with which she had put them around me as if she were repeating the empty and formal gesture of all promise so that I should never forget it, the elbows angling outwards as she put her hands to the sprig of verbena in her hair, I standing straight and rigid facing the slightly bent head, the short jagged hair, the rigid curiously formal angle of the bare arms gleaming faintly in the last of light as she removed the verbena sprig and put it into my lapel and I thought how the War had tried to stamp all the women of her generation and class in the South into a type and how it had failed – the suffering, the identical experience (hers and Aunt Jenny's had been almost the same except that Aunt Jenny had spent a few nights with her husband before they brought him back home in an ammunition wagon while Gavin Breckbridge was just Drusilla's fiancé) was there in the eyes, yet beyond that was the incorrigibly individual woman: not like so many men who return from wars to live on Government reservations like so many steers, emasculate and empty of all save an identical experience which they cannot forget and dare not, else they would cease to live at that moment, almost interchangeable save for the old habit of answering to a given name.

'Now I must tell Father,' I said.

'Yes,' she said. 'You must tell him. Kiss me.' So again it was like it had been before. No. Twice, a thousand times and never like – the eternal and symbolical thirty to a young man, a youth, each time both cumulative and retroactive, immitigably unrepetitive, each wherein remembering excludes experience, each wherein experience antedates remembering; the skill without weariness, the knowledge virginal to surfeit, the cunning secret muscles to guide and control just as within the wrists and elbows lay slumbering the mastery of horses: she stood back, already turning, not looking at me when she spoke, never having looked at me, already moving swiftly on in the dusk: 'Tell John. Tell him tonight.'

I intended to. I went to the house and into the office at once; I went to the centre of the rug before the cold hearth, I don't know why, and stood there rigid like soldiers stand, looking at eye level straight across the room and above his head and said 'Father' and then stopped. Because he did not even hear me. He said, 'Yes, Bayard?' but he did not hear me although he was sitting behind the desk doing nothing, immobile, as still as I was rigid, one hand on the desk with a dead cigar in it, a bottle of brandy and a filled and untasted glass beside his hand, clothed quiet and bemused in whatever triumph it was he felt since the last overwhelming return of votes had come in late in the afternoon. So I waited until after supper. We went to the dining-room and stood side by side until Aunt Jenny entered and then Drusilla, in the yellow ball gown, who walked straight to me and gave me one fierce inscrutable look then went to her place and waited for me to draw her chair while Father drew Aunt Jenny's. He had roused by then, not to talk himself but rather to sit at the head of the table and reply to Drusilla as she talked with a sort of feverish and glittering volubility – to reply now and then to her with that courteous intolerant pride which had lately become a little forensic, as if merely being in a political contest filled with fierce and empty oratory had retroactively made a lawyer of him who was anything and everything except a lawyer. Then Drusilla and Aunt Jenny rose and left us and he said 'Wait' to me who had made no move to follow and directed Joby to bring one of the bottles of wine which he had fetched back from New Orleans when he went there last to borrow money to liquidate his first private railroad bonds. Then I stood again like soldiers stand, gazing at eye level above his head while he sat half-turned from the table, a little paunchy now though not much, a little grizzled too in the hair though his beard was as strong as ever, with that spurious forensic air of lawyers and the intolerant eyes which in the last two years had acquired that transparent film which the eyes of carnivorous animals have and from behind which they look at a world which no ruminant ever sees, perhaps dares to see, which I have seen before on the eyes of men who have killed too much, who have killed so much that never again as long as they live will they ever be alone. I said again, 'Father' then I told him.

'Hah?' he said. 'Sit down.' I sat down, I looked at him, watched him fill both glasses and this time I knew it was worse with him than not hearing: it didn't even matter. 'You are doing well in the law, Judge Wilkins tells me. I am pleased to hear that. I have not needed you in my affairs so far, but from now on I shall. I have now accomplished the active portion of my aims in which you could not have helped me; I acted as the land and the time demanded and you were too young for that, I wished to shield you. But now the land and the time too are changing; what will follow will be a matter of consolidation, of pettifogging and doubtless chicanery in which I would be a babe in arms but in which you, trained in the law, can hold your own – our own. Yes, I have accomplished my aim, and now I shall do a little moral house-cleaning. I am tired of killing men, no matter what the necessity nor the end. Tomorrow, when I go to town and meet Ben Redmond, I shall be unarmed.'

3

We reached home just before midnight; we didn't have to pass through Jefferson either. Before we turned in the gates I could see the lights, the chandeliers – hall, parlour, and what Aunt

Jenny (without any effort or perhaps even design on her part)
had taught even Ringo to call the drawing-room, the light
falling outwards across the portico, past the columns. Then I
saw the horses, the faint shine of leather and buckle-glints on the
black silhouettes and then the men too – Wyatt and others of
Father's old troop – and I had forgot that they would be there.
I had forgot that they would be there; I remember how I
thought, since I was tired and spent with strain, *Now it will have
to begin tonight. I won't even have until tomorrow in which to begin to
resist*. They had a watchman, a picket out, I suppose, because
they seemed to know at once that we were in the drive. Wyatt
met me, I halted the mare, I could look down at him and at the
others gathered a few yards behind him with that curious vul-
ture-like formality which Southern men assume in such situa-
tions.

'Well, boy,' George said.

'Was it – ' I said. 'Was he – '

'It was all right. It was in front. Redmond ain't no coward.
John had the derringer inside his cuff like always, but he never
touched it, never made a move towards it.' I have seen him do
it, he showed me once: the pistol (it was not four inches long)
held flat inside his left wrist by a clip he made himself of wire
and an old clock spring; he would raise both hands at the same
time, cross them, fire the pistol from beneath his left hand
almost as if he were hiding from his own vision what he was
doing; when he killed one of the men he shot a hole through his
own coat sleeve. 'But you want to get on to the house,' Wyatt
said. He began to stand aside, then he spoke again: 'We'll take
this off your hands, any of us. Me.' I hadn't moved the mare yet
and I had made no move to speak, yet he continued quickly, as
if he had already rehearsed all this, his speech and mine, and
knew what I would say and only spoke himself as he would have
removed his hat on entering a house or used 'sir' in conversing
with a stranger: 'You're young, just a boy, you ain't had any
experience in this kind of thing. Besides, you got them two
ladies in the house to think about. He would understand, all
right.'

'I reckon I can attend to it,' I said.

'Sure,' he said; there was no surprise, nothing at all, in his voice because he had already rehearsed this: 'I reckon we all knew that's what you would say.' He stepped back then; almost it was as though he and not I bade the mare to move on. But they all followed, still with that unctuous and voracious formality. Then I saw Drusilla standing at the top of the front steps, in the light from the open door and the windows like a theatre scene, in the yellow ball gown and even from here I believed that I could smell the verbena in her hair, standing there motionless yet emanating something louder than the two shots must have been – something voracious too and passionate. Then, although I had dismounted and someone had taken the mare, I seemed to be still in the saddle and to watch myself enter that scene which she had postulated like another actor while in the background for chorus Wyatt and the others stood with the unctuous formality which the Southern man shows in the presence of death – that Roman holiday engendered by mist-born Protestantism grafted on to this land of violent sun, of violent alteration from snow to heat-stroke which has produced a race impervious to both. I mounted the steps towards the figure straight and yellow and immobile as a candle which moved only to extend one hand; we stood together and looked down at them where they stood clumped, the horses too gathered in a tight group beyond them at the rim of light from the brilliant door and windows. One of them stamped and blew his breath and jangled his gear.

'Thank you, gentlemen,' I said. 'My aunt and my – Drusilla thank you. There's no need for you to stay. Good night.' They murmured, turning. George Wyatt paused, looking back at me.

'Tomorrow?' he said.

'Tomorrow.' Then they went on, carrying their hats and tiptoeing, even on the ground, the quiet and resilient earth, as though anyone in that house awake would try to sleep, anyone already asleep in it whom they could have wakened. Then they were gone and Drusilla and I turned and crossed the portico, her hand lying light on my wrist yet discharging into me with a shock like electricity that dark and passionate voracity, the face at my shoulder – the jagged hair with a verbena sprig above each ear, the eyes staring at me with that fierce exaltation.

We entered the hall and crossed it, her hand guiding me without pressure, and entered the parlour. Then for the first time I realized it – the alteration which is death – not that he was now just clay but that he was lying down. But I didn't look at him yet because that when I did I would begin to pant; I went to Aunt Jenny who had just risen from a chair behind which Louvinia stood. She was Father's sister, taller than Drusilla but no older, whose husband had been killed at the very beginning of the War, by a shell from a Federal frigate at Fort Moultrie, come to us from Carolina six years ago. Ringo and I went to Tennessee Junction in the wagon to meet her. It was January, cold and clear and with ice in the ruts; we returned just before dark with Aunt Jenny on the seat beside me holding a lace parasol and Ringo in the wagon bed nursing a hamper basket containing two bottles of old sherry and the two jasmine cuttings which were bushes in the garden now, and the panes of coloured glass which she had salvaged from the Carolina house where she and Father and Uncle Bayard were born and which Father had set in a fanlight about one of the drawing-room windows for her – who came up the drive and Father (home now from the railroad) went down the steps and lifted her from the wagon and said, 'Well, Jenny,' and she said, 'Well, Johnny,' and began to cry. She stood too, looking at me as I approached – the same hair, the same high nose, the same eyes as Father's except that they were intent and very wise instead of intolerant. She said nothing at all, she just kissed me, her hands light on my shoulders. Then Drusilla spoke, as if she had been waiting with a sort of dreadful patience for the empty ceremony to be done, in a voice like a bell: clear, unsentient, on a single pitch, silvery and triumphant: 'Come, Bayard.'

'Hadn't you better go to bed now?' Aunt Jenny said.

'Yes,' Drusilla said in that silvery ecstatic voice, 'Oh yes. There will be plenty of time for sleep.' I followed her, her hand again guiding me without pressure; now I looked at him. It was just as I had imagined it – sabre, plumes, and all – but with that alteration, that irrevocable difference which I had known to expect yet had not realized, as you can put food into your stomach which for a while the stomach declines to assimilate – the illimitable grief and regret as I looked down at the face which I knew – the nose, the hair, the eyelids closed over the intolerance – the face which I realized I now saw in repose for the first time in my life; the empty hands still now beneath the invisible stain of what had been (once surely) needless blood, the hands now appearing clumsy in their very inertness, too clumsy to have performed the fatal actions which forever afterwards he must have waked and slept with and maybe was glad to lay down at last – those curious appendages clumsily conceived to begin with yet with which man has taught himself to do so much, so much more than they were intended to do or could be forgiven for doing, which had now surrendered that life to which his intolerant heart had fiercely held; and then I knew that in a minute I would begin to pant. So Drusilla must have spoken twice before I heard her and turned and saw in the instant Aunt Jenny and Louvinia watching us, hearing Drusilla now, the unsentient bell quality gone now, her voice whispering into that quiet death-filled room with a passionate and dying fall: 'Bayard.' She faced me, she was quite near; again the scent of the verbena in her hair seemed to have increased a hundred times as she stood holding out to me, one in either hand, the two duelling pistols. 'Take them, Bayard,' she said, in the same tone in which she had said 'Kiss me' last summer, already pressing them into my hands, watching me with that passionate and voracious exaltation, speaking in a voice fainting and passionate with promise: 'Take them. I have kept them for you. I give them to you. Oh you will thank me, you will remember me who put into your hands what they say is an attribute only of God's, who took what belongs to heaven and gave it to you. Do you feel them? the long true barrels true as justice, the triggers (you have fired them) quick as retribution, the two of them slender and invincible and fatal as the physical shape of love?' Again I watched her arms angle out and upwards as she removed the two verbena sprigs from her hair in two motions faster than the eye could follow, already putting one of them into my lapel and crushing the other in her other hand while she still spoke in that rapid passionate voice not much louder than a whisper: 'There. One I give to you to wear tomorrow (it will not fade), the other I cast away, like this –' dropping the crushed bloom at her feet. 'I abjure it. I abjure verbena forever more; I have smelled it above the odour of courage; that was all I wanted. Now let me look at you.' She stood back, staring at me – the face tearless and exalted, the feverish eyes brilliant and voracious. 'How beautiful you are: do you know it? How beautiful: young, to be permitted to kill, to be permitted vengeance, to take into your bare hands the fire of heaven that cast down Lucifer. No; I. I gave it to you; I put it into your hands; Oh you will thank me, you will remember me when I am dead and you are an old man saying to himself, "I have tasted all things." – It will be the right hand, won't it?' She moved; she had taken my right hand which still held one of the pistols before I knew what she was about to do; she had bent and kissed it before I comprehended why she took it. Then she stopped dead still, still stopping in that attitude of fierce exultant humility, her hot lips and her hot hands still touching my flesh, light on my flesh as dead leaves yet communicating to it that battery charge dark, passionate and damned forever of all peace. Because they are wise, women are – a touch, lips or fingers, and the knowledge, even clair-voyance, goes straight to the heart without bothering the laggard brain at all. She stood erect now, staring at me with intolerable and amazed incredulity which occupied her face alone for a whole minute while her eyes were completely empty; it seemed to me that I stood there for a full minute while Aunt Jenny and Louvinia watched us, waiting for her eyes to fill. There was no blood in her face at all, her mouth open a little and pale as one of those rubber rings women seal fruit jars with. Then her eyes filled with an expression of bitter and passionate betrayal. 'Why, he's not –' she said. 'He's not – And I kissed his hand,' she said in an aghast whisper; '*I kissed his hand*!' beginning to laugh, the laughter, rising, becoming a scream yet still remaining laughter, screaming with laughter, trying herself to deaden the sound by putting her hand over her mouth, the laughter spilling between her fingers like vomit, the incredulous betrayed eyes still watching me across the hand.

'Louvinia!' Aunt Jenny said. They both came to her. Louvinia touched and held her and Drusilla turned her face to Louvinia.

'I kissed his hand, Louvinia!' she cried. 'Did you see it? *I kissed his hand*!' the laughter rising again, becoming the scream again yet still remaining laughter, she still trying to hold it back with her hand like a small child who has filled its mouth to full.

'Take her upstairs,' Aunt Jenny said. But they were already moving towards the door, Louvinia half-carrying Drusilla, the laughter diminishing as they neared the door as though it waited for the larger space of the empty and brilliant hall to rise again. Then it was gone; Aunt Jenny and I stood there and I knew that soon, I would begin to pant. I could feel it beginning like you feel regurgitation beginning, as though there were not enough air in the room, the house, not enough air anywhere under the heavy hot low sky where the equinox couldn't seem to accomplish, nothing in the air for breathing, for the lungs. Now it was Aunt Jenny who said 'Bayard' twice before I heard her. 'You are not going to try to kill him. All right.'

'All right?' I said.

'Yes. All right. Don't let it be Drusilla, a poor hysterical young woman. And don't let it be him, Bayard, because he's dead now. And don't let it be George Wyatt and those others who will be waiting for you tomorrow morning. I know you are not afraid.'

'But what good will that do?' I said. 'What good will that do?' It almost began then; I stopped it just in time. 'I must live with myself, you see.'

'Then it's not just Drusilla? Not just him? Not just George Wyatt and Jefferson?'

'No,' I said.

'Will you promise to let me see you before you go to town tomorrow?' I looked at her; we looked at one another for a moment. Then she put her hands on my shoulders and kissed me and released me, all in one motion. 'Good night, son,' she said. Then she was gone too and now it could begin. I knew that in a minute I would look at him and it would begin and I did look at him, feeling the long-held breath, the hiatus before it started, thinking how maybe I should have said, 'Good-bye, Father' but did not. Instead I crossed to the piano and laid the pistols carefully on it, still keeping the panting from getting too loud too soon. Then I was outside on the porch and (I don't know how long it had been) I looked in the window and saw

Simon squatting on a stool beside him. Simon had been his
body servant during the War and when they came home Simon
had a uniform too – a Confederate private's coat with a Yankee
brigadier's star on it and he had put it on now too, like they had
dressed Father, squatting on the stool beside him, not crying,
not weeping the facile tears which are the white man's futile
trait and which Negroes know nothing about but just sitting
there, motionless, his lower lip slacked down a little; he raised
his hand and touched the coffin, the black hand rigid and fragile-
looking as a clutch of dead twigs, then dropped the hand; once
he turned his head and I saw his eyes roll red and unwinking in
his skull like those of a cornered fox. It had begun by that time;
I panted, standing there, and this was it – the regret and grief,
the despair out of which the tragic mute insensitive bones stand
up that can bear anything, anything.

4

After a while the whippoorwills stopped and I heard the first
day bird, a mockingbird. It had sung all night too but now it
was the day song, no longer the drowsy moony fluting. Then
they all began – the sparrows from the stable, the thrush that
lived in Aunt Jenny's garden, and I heard a quail too from the
pasture and now there was light in the room. But I didn't move
at once. I still lay on the bed (I hadn't undressed) with my hands
under my head and the scent of Drusilla's verbena faint from
where my coat lay on a chair, watching the light grow, watching
it turn rosy with the sun. After a while I heard Louvinia come
up across the back yard and go into the kitchen; I heard the
door and then the long crash of her armful of stovewood into
the box. Soon they would begin to arrive – the carriages and
buggies in the drive – but not for a while yet because they too
would wait first to see what I was going to do. So the house was
quiet when I went down to the dining-room, no sound in it
except Simon snoring in the parlour, probably still sitting on
the stool though I didn't look in to see. Instead I stood at the
dining-room window and drank the coffee which Louvinia
brought me, then I went to the stable; I saw Joby watching me
from the kitchen door as I crossed the yard and in the stable

Loosh looked up at me across Betsy's head, a curry comb in his hand, though Ringo didn't look at me at all. We curried Jupiter then. I didn't know if we would be able to without trouble or not, since always Father would come in first and touch him and tell him to stand and he would stand like a marble horse (or pale bronze rather) while Loosh curried him. But he stood for me too, a little restive but he stood, then that was done and now it was almost nine o'clock and soon they would begin to arrive and I told Ringo to bring Betsy on to the house.

I went on to the house and into the hall. I had not had to pant in some time now but it was there, waiting, a part of the alteration, as though by being dead and no longer needing air he had taken all of it, all that he had compassed and claimed and postulated between the walls which he had built, along with him. Aunt Jenny must have been waiting; she came out of the dining-room at once, without a sound, dressed, the hair that was like Father's combed and smooth above the eyes that were different from Father's eyes because they were not intolerant but just intent and grave and (she was wise too) without pity. 'Are you going now?' she said.

'Yes.' I looked at her. Yes, thank God, without pity. 'You see, I want to be thought well of.'

'I do,' she said. 'Even if you spend the day hidden in the stable loft, I still do.'

'Maybe if she knew that I was going. Was going to town anyway.'

'No,' she said. 'No, Bayard.' We looked at one another. Then she said quietly, 'All right. She's awake.' So I mounted the stairs. I mounted steadily, not fast because if I had gone fast the panting would have started again or I might have had to slow for a second at the turn or at the top and I would not have gone on. So I went slowly and steadily, across the hall to her door and knocked and opened it. She was sitting at the window, in something soft and loose for morning in her bedroom, only she never did look like morning in a bedroom because there was no hair to fall about her shoulders. She looked up, she sat there looking at me with her feverish brilliant eyes and I remembered I still had the verbena sprig in my lapel and suddenly she began to laugh again. It seemed to

167

come not from her mouth but to burst out all over her face like sweat does and with a dreadful and painful convulsion as when you have vomited until it hurts you yet still you must vomit again – burst out all over her face except her eyes, the brilliant incredulous eyes looking at me out of the laughter as if they belonged to somebody else, as if they were two inert fragments of tar or coal lying on the bottom of a receptacle filled with turmoil: 'I kissed his hand! *I kissed his hand*!' Louvinia entered, Aunt Jenny must have sent her directly after me; again I walked slowly and steadily so it would not start yet, down the stairs where Aunt Jenny stood beneath the chandelier in the hall as Mrs Wilkins had stood yesterday at the University. She had my hat in her hand. 'Even if you hid all day in the stable, Bayard,' she said. I took the hat; she said quietly, pleasantly, as if she were talking to a stranger, a guest: 'I used to see a lot of block-ade runners in Charleston. They were heroes in a way, you see – not heroes because they were helping to prolong the Con-federacy but heroes in the sense that David Crockett or John Sevier would have been to small boys or fool young women. There was one of them, an Englishman. He had no business there; it was the money of course, as with all of them. But he was the Davy Crockett to us because by that time we had all forgot what money was, what you could do with it. He must have been a gentleman once or associated with gentlemen before he changed his name, and he had a vocabulary of seven words, though I must admit he got along quite well with them. The first four were, "I'll have rum, thanks," and then, when he had the rum, he would use the other three – across the cham-pagne, to whatever ruffled bosom or low gown: "No bloody moon." No bloody moon, Bayard.'

Ringo was waiting with Betsy at the front steps. Again he did not look at me, his face sullen, downcast even while he handed me the reins. But he said nothing, nor did I look back. And sure enough I was just in time; I passed the Compson carriage at the gates, General Compson lifted his hat as I did mine as we passed. It was four miles to town but I had not gone two of them when I heard the horse coming up behind me and I did not look back because I knew it was Ringo. I did not look back; he came up on one of the carriage horses, he rode up beside me and looked me full in the face for one moment, the sullen determined face, the eyes rolling at me defiant and momentary and red; we rode on. Now we were in town – the long shady street leading to the square, the new courthouse at the end of it; it was eleven o'clock now: long past breakfast and not yet noon so there were only women on the street, not to recognize me perhaps or at least not the walking stopped sudden and dead in midwalking as if the legs contained the sudden eyes, the caught breath, that not to begin until we reached the square and I thinking *If I could only be invisible until I reach the stairs to his office and begin to mount*. But I could not; I was not; we rode up to the Holston House and I saw the row of feet along the gallery rail come suddenly and quietly down and I did not look at them, I stopped Betsy and waited until Ringo was down then I dismounted and gave him the reins. 'Wait for me here,' I said.

'I'm going with you,' he said, not loud; we stood there under the still circumspect eyes and spoke quietly to one another like two conspirators. Then I saw the pistol, the outline of it inside his shirt, probably the one we had taken from Grumby that day we killed him.

'No you ain't,' I said.

'Yes I am.'

'No you ain't.' So I walked on, along the street in the hot sun. It was almost noon now and I could smell nothing except the verbena in my coat, as if it had gathered all the sun, all the suspended fierce heat in which the equinox could not seem to occur and were distilling it so that I moved in a cloud of verbena as I might have moved in a cloud of smoke from a cigar. Then George Wyatt was beside me (I don't know where he came from) and five or six others of Father's old troop a few yards behind, George's hand on my arm, drawing me into a doorway out of the avid eyes like caught breaths.

'Have you got that derringer?' George said.

'No,' I said.

'Good,' George said. 'They are tricky things to fool with. Couldn't nobody but Colonel ever handle one right; I never could. So you take this. I tried it this morning and I know it's right. Here.' He was already fumbling the pistol into my pocket, then the same thing seemed to happen to him that happened to

Drusilla last night when she kissed my hand – something com-
municated by touch straight to the simple code by which he
lived, without going through the brain at all: so that he too
stood suddenly back, the pistol in his hand, staring at me with
his pale outraged eyes and speaking in a whisper thin with fury:
'Who are you? Is your name Sartoris? By God, if you don't
kill him, I'm going to.' Now it was not panting, it was a terrible
desire to laugh, to laugh as Drusilla had, and say, 'That's what
Drusilla said.' But I didn't, I said,

'I'm tending to this. You stay out of it. I don't need any
help.' Then his fierce eyes faded gradually, exactly as you turn
a lamp down.

'Well,' he said, putting the pistol back into his pocket.
'You'll have to excuse me, son. I should have knowed you
wouldn't do anything that would keep John from laying quiet.
We'll follow you and wait at the foot of the steps. And remember: he's a brave man, but he's been sitting in that office by
himself since yesterday morning waiting for you and his nerves
are on edge.'

'I'll remember,' I said. 'I don't need any help.' I had started
on when suddenly I said it without having any warning that I
was going to: 'No bloody moon.'

'What?' he said. I didn't answer. I went on across the square
itself now, in the hot sun, they following though not close so
that I never saw them again until afterwards, surrounded by
the remote still eyes not following me yet either, just stopped
where they were before the stores and about the door to the
courthouse, waiting. I walked steadily on enclosed in the now
fierce odour of the verbena sprig. Then shadow fell upon me; I
did not pause, I looked once at the small faded sign nailed to
the brick, *B. J. Redmond. Atty at Law* and began to mount the
stairs, the wooden steps scuffed by the heavy bewildered boots
of countrymen approaching litigation and stained by tobacco
spit, on down the dim corridor to the door which bore the
name again, *B. J. Redmond* and knocked once and opened it. He
sat behind the desk, not much taller than Father but thicker as
a man gets who spends most of his time sitting and listening to
people, freshly shaven and with fresh linen; a lawyer yet it was
not a lawyer's face – a face much thinner than the body would

indicate, strained (and yes, tragic; I know that now) and exhausted beneath the neat recent steady strokes of the razor, holding a pistol flat on the desk before him, loose beneath his hand and aimed at nothing. There was no smell of drink, not even of tobacco in the neat clean dingy room although I knew he smoked. I didn't pause. I walked steadily towards him. It was not twenty feet from door to desk yet I seemed to walk in a dreamlike state in which there was neither time nor distance, as though the mere act of walking was no more intended to encompass space than was his sitting. We didn't speak. It was as if we both knew what the passage of words would be and the futility of it; how he might have said, 'Go out, Bayard. Go away, boy' and then, 'Draw then. I will allow you to draw' and it would have been the same as if he had never said it. So we did not speak; I just walked steadily towards him as the pistol rose from the desk. I watched it, I could see the foreshortened slant of the barrel and I knew it would miss me though his hand did not tremble. I walked towards him, towards the pistol in the rocklike hand, I heard no bullet. Maybe I didn't even hear the explosion though I remember the sudden orange bloom and smoke as they appeared against his white shirt as they had appeared against Grumby's greasy Confederate coat; I still watched that foreshortened slant of barrel which I knew was not aimed at me and saw the second orange flash and smoke and heard no bullet that time either. Then I stopped; it was done then. I watched the pistol descend to the desk in short jerks; I saw him release it and sit back, both hands on the desk, I looked at his face and I knew too what it was to want air when there was nothing in the circumambience for the lungs. He rose, shoved the chair back with a convulsive motion and rose, with a queer ducking motion of his head; with his head still ducked aside and one arm extended as though he couldn't see and the other hand resting on the desk as if he couldn't stand alone, he turned and crossed to the wall and took his hat from the rack and with his head still ducked aside and one hand extended he blundered along the wall and passed me and reached the door and went through it. He was brave; no one denied that. He walked down those stairs and out on to the street where George Wyatt and the other six of Father's old troop waited and where the other men had begun to run now; he walked through the middle of them with his hat on and his head up (they told me how someone shouted at him: 'Have you killed that boy too?'), saying no word, staring straight ahead and with his back to them, on to the station where the south-bound train was just in and got on it with no baggage, nothing, and went away from Jefferson and from Mississippi and never came back.

I heard their feet on the stairs then in the corridor then in the room, but for a while yet (it wasn't that long, of course) I still sat behind the desk as he had sat, the flat of the pistol still warm under my hand, my hand growing slowly numb between the pistol and my forehead. Then I raised my head; the little room was full of men. 'My God!' George Wyatt cried. 'You took the pistol away from him and then missed him, missed him *twice*?' Then he answered himself – that same rapport for violence which Drusilla had and which in George's case was actual character judgement: 'No; wait. You walked in here without even a pocket knife and let him miss you twice. My God in heaven.' He turned, shouting: 'Get to hell out of here! You, White, ride out to Sartoris and tell his folks it's all over and he's all right. Ride!' So they departed, went away; presently only George was left, watching me with that pale bleak stare which was speculative yet not at all ratiocinative. 'Well by God,' he said. '– Do you want a drink?'

'No,' I said. 'I'm hungry. I didn't eat any breakfast.'

'I reckon not, if you got up this morning aiming to do what you did. Come on. We'll go to the Holston House.'

'No,' I said. 'No. Not there.'

'Why not? You ain't done anything to be ashamed of. I wouldn't have done it that way myself. I'd a shot at him once, anyway. But that's your way or you wouldn't have done it.'

'Yes,' I said. 'I would do it again.'

'Be damned if I would – You want to come home with me? We'll have time to eat and then ride out there in time for the –' But I couldn't do that either.

'No,' I said. 'I'm not hungry after all. I think I'll go home.'

'Don't you want to wait and ride out with me?'

'No. I'll go on.'

'You don't want to stay here, anyway,' He looked around the room again, where the smell of powder smoke still lingered a little, still lay somewhere on the hot dead air though invisible now, blinking a little with his fierce pale unintroverted eyes. 'Well by God,' he said again. 'Maybe you're right, maybe there has been enough killing in your family without – Come on.' We left the office. I waited at the foot of the stairs and soon Ringo came up with the horses. We crossed the square again. There were no feet on the Holston House railing now (it was twelve o'clock) but a group of men stood before the door who raised their hats and I raised mine and Ringo and I rode on.

We did not go fast. Soon it was one, maybe after; the carriages and buggies would begin to leave the square soon, so I turned from the road at the end of the pasture and I sat the mare, trying to open the gate without dismounting, until Ringo dismounted and opened it. We crossed the pasture in the hard fierce sun; I could have seen the house now but I didn't look. Then we were in the shade, the close thick airless shade of the creek bottom; the old rails still lay in the undergrowth where we had built the pen to hide the Yankee mules. Presently I heard the water, then I could see the sunny glints. We dismounted. I lay on my back, I thought *Now it can begin again if it wants to.* But it did not. I went to sleep. I went to sleep almost before I had stopped thinking. I slept for almost five hours and I didn't dream anything at all yet I waked myself up crying, crying too hard to stop it. Ringo was squatting beside me and the sun was gone though there was a bird of some sort still singing somewhere and the whistle of the north-bound evening train sounded and the short broken puffs of starting where it had evidently stopped at our flag station. After a while I began to stop and Ringo brought his hat full of water from the creek but instead I went down to the water myself and bathed my face.

There was still a good deal of light in the pasture, though the whippoorwills had begun, and when we reached the house there was a mockingbird singing in the magnolia, the night song now, the drowsy moony one, and again the moon like the rim print of a heel in wet sand. There was just one light in the hall now and so it was all over though I could still smell the flowers even above the verbena in my coat. I had not looked at him again. I had started to before I left the house but I did not, I did not see him again and all the pictures we had of him were bad ones because a picture could no more have held him dead than the house could have kept his body. But I didn't need to see him again because he was there, he would always be there; maybe what Drusilla meant by his dream was not something which he possessed but something which he had bequeathed us which we could never forget, which would even assume the corporeal shape of him whenever any of us, black or white, closed our eyes. I went into the house. There was no light in the drawing-room except the last of the afterglow which came through the western window where Aunt Jenny's coloured glass was; I was about to go on upstairs when I saw her sitting there beside the window. She didn't call me and I didn't speak Drusilla's name, I just went to the door and stood there. 'She's gone,' Aunt Jenny said. 'She took the evening train. She has gone to Montgomery, to Dennison.' Denny had been married about a year now; he was living in Montgomery, reading law.

'I see,' I said. 'Then she didn't – ' But there wasn't any use in that either; Jed White must have got there before one o'clock and told them. And besides, Aunt Jenny didn't answer. She could have lied to me but she didn't, she said,

'Come here.' I went to her chair. 'Kneel down. I can't see you.'

'Don't you want the lamp?'

'No. Kneel down.' So I knelt beside the chair. 'So you had a perfectly splendid Saturday afternoon, didn't you? Tell me about it.' Then she put her hands on my shoulders. I watched them come up as though she were trying to stop them; I felt them on my shoulders as if they had a separate life of their own and were trying to do something which for my sake she was trying to restrain, prevent. Then she gave up or she was not strong enough because they came up and took my face between them, hard, and suddenly the tears sprang and streamed down her face like Drusilla's laughing had. 'Oh, damn you Sartorises!' she said. 'Damn you! Damn you!'

As I passed down the hall the light came up in the dining-room and I could hear Louvinia laying the table for supper. So the stairs were lighted quite well. But the upper hall was dark.

I saw her open door (that unmistakable way in which an open door stands open when nobody lives in the room any more) and I realized I had not believed that she was really gone. So I didn't look into the room. I went on to mine and entered. And then for a long moment I thought it was the verbena in my lapel which I still smelled. I thought that until I had crossed the room and looked down at the pillow on which it lay – the single sprig of it (without looking she would pinch off a half dozen of them and they would be all of a size, almost all of a shape, as if a machine had stamped them out) filling the room, the dusk, the evening with that odour which she said you could smell alone above the smell of horses.

WILLIAM FAULKNER

GO DOWN, MOSES

The seven dramatic stories in this volume show this great writer's compassionate understanding of the Negro world of the Deep South.

'Has a richness of colour and feeling that belongs to maturity . . . exceptional wisdom and sympathy' – *Observer*

INTRUDER IN THE DUST

This novel is, in effect, a thriller, but is intimately concerned with racialism and the status of the Negro. Faulkner was himself a Southerner.

'A very good novel indeed' – John Betjeman

LIGHT IN AUGUST

Once described as a 'macabre fantasy' and, again, as an 'epileptic fit', *Light in August* has now come to be seen as an American literary landmark.

'Burns throughout with a fierce indignation against cruelty, stupidity, and prejudice . . . a great book' – *Spectator*

Also published

Absalom, Absalom!
The Reivers
Soldiers' Pay
As I Lay Dying
Sanctuary
The Sound and the Fury
Requiem for a Nun
The Wild Palms